ASTEROID 6
AND OTHER TALES OF COSMIC HORROR

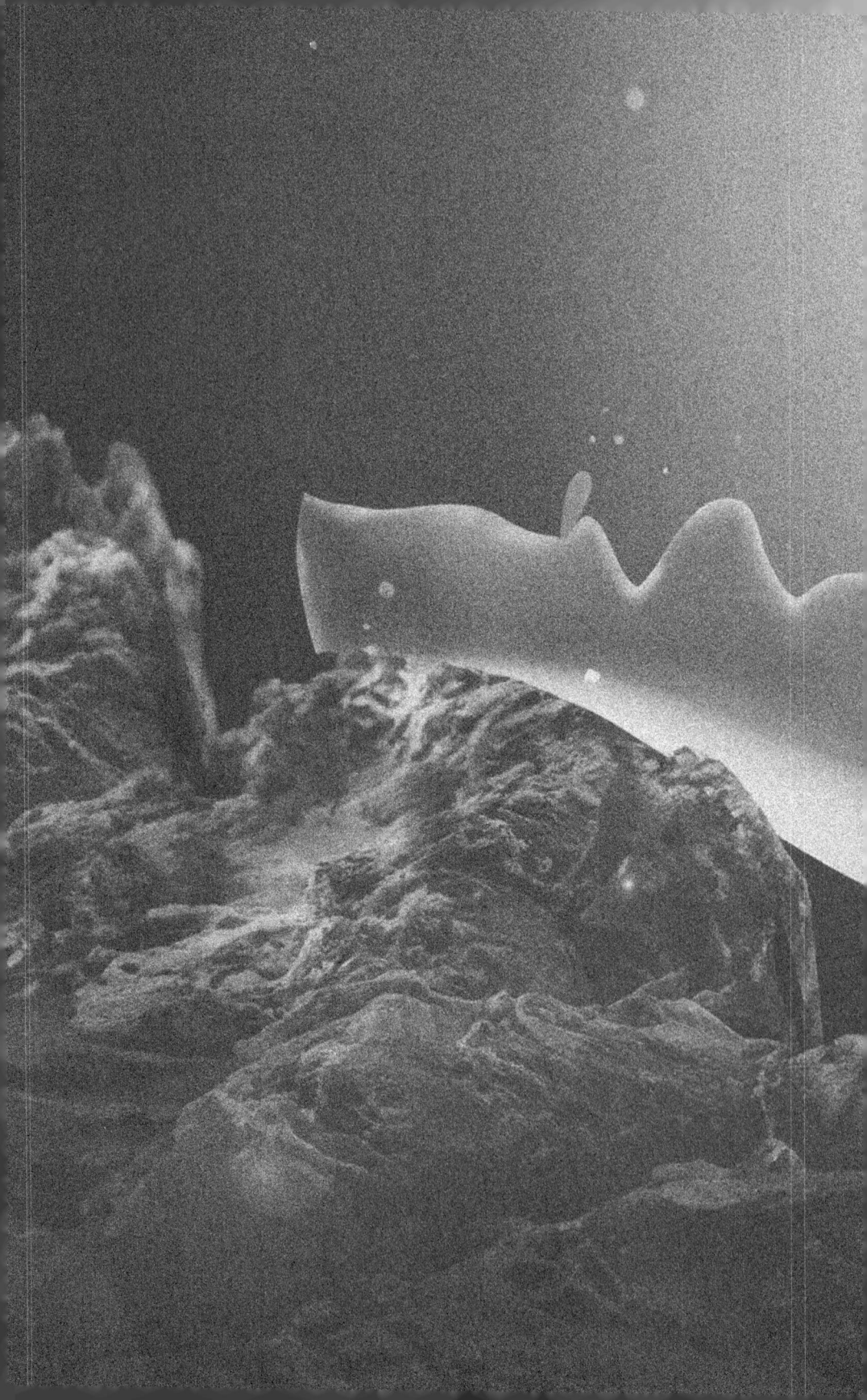

ASTEROID 6
AND OTHER TALES OF COSMIC HORROR

R. DAVID FULCHER

GRAVELIGHT PRESS | LOS ANGELES

ASTEROID 6
AND OTHER TALES OF COSMIC HORROR

Copyright ©2024 R. David Fulcher. All rights reserved.
Published by Gravelight Press, an imprint of
Current Words Publishing, LLC, Dianne Pearce, publisher.
Cover and design copyright @2024 David Yurkovich.
Editing: Dianne Pearce
Proofreading: Angela Walker

This is a work of fiction. Any similarities between actual persons, events, places, things, ghosts, goblins, specters, etcetera are strictly coincidental.
So say we all.

The following stories were previously published: "The Bogeyman, Pt. II" originally appeared in *Three-Lobed Burning Eye* magazine, *Annual 1*. Copyright ©1991 by R. David Fulcher. "The Witch Toaster" originally appeared in *Forging Freedom: Dimensions*. Copyright ©2014 R. David Fulcher. "Madame Zeist's Perfume" first appeared as an online publication at Val Muller: The Electronic Wordsmith (valmuller.com/blog). Copyright ©2018 R. David Fulcher. All works appearing in this collection have been revised from their originally published versions.

ISBN: 978-1-957224-39-8

gravelightpress.com | currentwords.com

DEDICATION

To my wife Lisa,
my moon and stars.
May we shine brightly
together forever.

ALSO BY R. DAVID FULCHER

FICTION

The Pumpkin King and Other Tales of Terror

Trains to Nowhere and Other Stories of World War II

Blood Spiders and Dark Moon, Tales of Horror,
Science Fiction and Fantasy

The Cemetery of Hearts, More Stories of Horror,
Fantasy and Science Fiction

The Lighthouse at Montauk Point and Other Stories

NONFICTION

The Movies That Make You Scream!

CONTENTS

The Outer Reaches of Unknown Kadaath 13

Asteroid 6 15

The Bogeyman, Pt. II 21

Electric 25

Club Mitternacht 33

The Witch Toaster 39

The Land Spider 45

Harley's Case 51

Madame Zeist's Perfume 55

Coming of Age 59

The Day of the Cricket 63

The Shamblers 67

Lawn Care 73

ASTEROID 6
AND OTHER TALES OF COSMIC HORROR

THE OUTER REACHES OF UNKNOWN KADAATH

Who would've thought
That H.P. was right
The Old Ones they beckon
Through the nebular night

Those in suspension
Suffocate in sleep
Yog-Sothooth promised
His secret to keep

The terminals flicker
The life support hums
The engines propel me
From the touch of our sun

Soon I will sleep,
Dreaming of the Mountains of Madness and the door
  behind the Silver Key
The end of mankind to be unlocked—
By one spaceship and me

ASTEROID 6

Asteroid clearing was always a bad duty. Jones sighed as he looked out into the dark void of space. The star combine continued its work, sweeping a cone-shaped field of energy out in front of the ship and turning this section of the Anterra asteroid belt into stardust.

Wilkes was somewhere in the back looking for beverage packets. He probably didn't even hear the proximity alert when it sounded. *Piece of crap,* thought Jones, kicking the console. The older combines, such as the *Starshine Boogie,* were notorious for malfunctioning.

But then Jones received visual confirmation.

The asteroid looming before him turned the cockpit of the small craft into shadow. It was the size of a small planet, far larger than anything the combine could handle. Jones rubbed his eyes and blinked several times to confirm. Sometimes, out in the belts on long shifts, space played tricks with your eyes. *Besides,* he wondered, *how could such a mammoth chunk of stone elude the long-range scanners?*

"Warning... current course obstructed..." droned the computer.

Wilkes grabbed the doorframe leading to the cockpit with two packets of Mango Poppers! in his free hand. "What the hell!" he exclaimed.

"Strap up," Jones ordered. "We're going to hit!"

Wilkes slid into the copilot's chair and buckled his reentry harness.

They activated the crash shield and lowered the shutter on the front portal. Each bore an uneasy expression. Wilkes tried to grin but the forced nature of the expression gave it an insane aspect that made Jones feel worse.

For a moment there was silence but for the strobe-like hum of the combine's matter disintegrator.

The impact was tremendous. The ship landed on the front right side and flipped over twice before settling on its roof.

The only sound Jones could hear was his own breath. He looked over at Wilkes, whose harnessed body hung limp, the pulp-like right side of his head crushed. His left hand was closed so tightly around the Mango Poppers! that the packaging was now torn. Syrupy orange juice covered Wilkes's chest. To Jones, it looked like alien blood.

Panic ensued, and Jones furiously fished for the harness release. After long moments, the latch clicked open and the restraining strap snapped back into its retractor housing. Jones tumbled out of the seat to the floor, which he soon realized was the roof. He also became aware that the asteroid had more gravity than expected. He scrambled to the control console and yanked the red lever, activating the ship's emergency transmitter. In approximately twelve hours, a company-issued rescue craft would arrive, and there was plenty of vitamin gel to sustain Jones while he waited.

Jones sat down on the roof and planned to spend the lonely hours feeling sorry for himself. He didn't succeed.

At first Jones thought that the darkness and isolation were causing him to hallucinate, but there was no denying the sounds that grew louder by the minute—a sweet and fragile crooning, like a choir of angels, but layered with undercurrents of strength and savagery. Jones suddenly realized that he wasn't hearing a signal across the vast vacuum of space. Rather, he felt the sound resonate within his own body—a direct transmission from nearby that reached directly into his skull and rattled his bones.

As if on autopilot, Jones clumsily crawled his way over the previously stowed equipment to the rear of the craft and donned a space suit.

Soon he was free, taking great, nearly weightless strides across the cratered surface toward the source of the sound. The number of abandoned spacecraft on the surface was surprising—mineral huskers, fighters from the Cimalyan War, and early-model star combines.

The song continued its intensity as he bounded ahead. Under normal conditions, Jones would have been concerned about escaping the asteroid's gravitational pull with his wild arcs, but he felt strangely secure and was determined to reach his goal.

Finally, he crossed a ridge and experienced a sensation not unlike desire as he spied a monolith in the distance. Ankh-like glyphs were carved into the pyramid's surface, and a green glow showed through the carvings, pulsing in time with the mesmerizing siren song.

As he moved closer, Jones realized how small and insignificant he was against the massive black pyramid. The cold bite of fear and isolation engulfed him. *It's going to be a long twelve hours,* he thought. He considered turning back, but the song intensified to the point of a scream. It drove him to his knees on the rocky ground.

I am your mother! the alien voice shrieked, outraged by Jones's attempt to resist his maker. *I am your wholeness!*

Driven to all fours by the sound, Jones bowed, supplicant.

The voice faded and Jones recovered his footing as a state of calm washed across his nervous system. The fear was gone, and once again, he felt the excitement he'd experienced upon seeing the monolith. It was as if he had never heard the shrieking voice. A hexagonal portal on each side of the monolith opened, welcomed him to enter the darkness. He moved fast.

Inside, Jones followed glowing runes toward the heart of the structure. The voice came again, welcoming now, and silently imparted to him the knowledge of the race that had created this pyramid, the glorious race that preexisted man and all of the creatures of the earth. The voice placed in his mind beautiful images of fantastic cities whose spires climbed upward to kiss pink moons and dark-winged creatures that braved the chrome skies.

Placing a gloved hand to what Jones thought of now as the breathing wall revealed images of the ancient race: slender, nearly nine feet tall, and possessed of strong features. Their laughter and speech hung in the crystalline air like notes of heavenly music above the atmospheric terraces and walkways of their cities. He witnessed lovemaking rituals that were sexual but not quite sex in human terms and the prows of black warships pushing through dark seas.

The wall repelled his touch and he could see no more. Jones felt hollow after breaking contact and continued along the dark corridor in search of connection. The tunnel began to slope steeply downward toward the center of the asteroid itself.

The channel cut down and down, on and on. Jones did not know how long he'd walked, but he was sweating profusely. When he felt hunger or fatigue, he would reach out to the glyphs and the monolith would replenish him, cool him, give him the will to continue.

Finally, he reached a cavernous hollow. The back walls of the chamber contained hexagonal sections like the honeycombs of a beehive. As Jones entered, the apiaries emitted a soft glow, and he could see that each chamber contained a member of the old race, curled on their sides as if in gentle sleep. They were suspended in their rest in a viscous solution that held them in stasis, hundreds vertically stacked into a shaft that extended above into the dark, a long tower of cells reaching up beyond Jones's vision.

A large black triangular-shaped spacecraft rested on the stone floor before the honeycombs. The chamber was divided in two by a sapphire-emerald energy field in the foreground. Jones felt agony upon realizing that the barrier kept him from the Old Ones. He stepped forward anyway. He needed to reach them, to be closer. As he advanced, his eyes were drawn to the black glow of an obsidian triangle set into the rock wall.

Release us! a thousand voices cried in unison within Jones's very soul.

As Jones raced toward the triangle, he tripped on something unseen and fell forward, slamming gloved hands against the rock floor. Someone or something—an arm—was now draped around his back. The scream he emitted was deafening but he could not escape his helmet to be heard. Jones struggled to free himself and stand.

It was then that he noticed the spacesuits littering the floor. *Ghost suits!* his mind yelled out, for each contained skeletal remains. The pressure suits bore the insignias of almost every planet in the Federation. The realization was as stark as it was certain: So many before him, from countless worlds, had come here to die.

Jones turned in horror toward the entrance where two creatures now stood in hostile, disciplined poses, features sharp and lean like their masters'. They were an amalgam of hound and gazelle as if manufactured in Dr. Moreau's South Pacific laboratory. Each sentinel stood six feet tall in chrome with azure stripes and muscles that rippled like gallium-indium eutectic.

They are the guardians, watchers of the gate! They will not harm you! the voices cried. *Release us! You are the chosen! You are the savior! The others were destroyers, but you are whom we have sought! Free us, and we will free the world!*

The emerald eyes of the guardians sparkled hypnotically at Jones in reassurance of this promise.

His terror subsided at their words, and Jones yearned once again to free the beautiful ones. He made his way in a rush toward the panel on the wall. Unintentionally, Jones brushed an elbow against the glowing barrier. Within a millisecond, a final series of images filled his mind in shocking brilliance. He saw the human colonies ablaze, the Old Ones cutting down the cities of Earth like mere weeds while their dark warships sailed unchallenged on hazy, blood-soaked tides. The eyes of the guardians lost their jeweled aspect as their lips tightened to reveal razor teeth.

This had been their plan all along: to find a specimen capable of reawakening them so that they might resume the carnage that the enslavement had denied them for so long. The guardians were there to punish him unless he did their bidding. It was all too clear, Jones realized, for he could not outlast them, certainly not for the twelve-hour period until, and if, he was found by the rescue team. Even if he managed to resist the call of the voices and the torture of the guardians, even if he was able to keep the dark creatures entombed, he would need to warn the rescue team to also resist the siren song.

Jones smiled back at the guardians, first in reassurance as he raised his hand toward the triangle set into the wall. In defiance, he suddenly released the oxygen seal of his helmet and, in his last moments of life, threw it across the floor, past the guardians, and into the passageway, a grim warning of those who might seek to save him. *Perhaps,* he thought, *it will be enough.* Within seconds his body folded in on itself and he collapsed to the ground, joining the rest of humanity's bones on the floor.

Unmoved in their chrysalis, the ethereal voices shrieked a final time—an audible cry that raced up the walls of the cavern and shook the bodies of Jones and his predecessors. With Jones's demise, no one remained to care for or help free the creatures. They would, for now at least, remain alone: an inert and impotent race, captives of Asteroid 6.

THE BOGEYMAN, PT. II

"Mother? Mom?" I cried out into the darkness. The hands of the clock on the nightstand read 9:05. My legs were pulled up to my chest, bunching up the sheets.

The next moments were awful, with just me holding my breath while beyond the closet door, the Bogeyman made his horrible noises. I was afraid I would wet myself. Again. Finally, Mom arrived.

The door opened a crack, but even that was enough to let in a triangular swath of yellow light. The border between my bed and the closet was once again a safe zone.

"What's the matter, dear?" she asked. Her voice helped me to think of other things—cotton candy and ice cream, kites at the beach, Christmas gifts.

"It's the Bogeyman. He's back again!" I said, breathing fast and quick.

She entered the room and sat at the bedside. Her dry hands grasped onto my sweaty hands. "Oh, Charlie. I thought I told you the Bogeyman was just a fairy tale."

"He's real! I can hear him. He waits until I'm alone, until the lights are out."

Mom stood up suddenly. "Is he in here, Charlie? Do you want me to open the closet and scare him away?"

"No!" I cried out.

"Please, Charlie, get some sleep. Tomorrow's a school day."

She sat down again and messed up my hair. I know I'm supposed to be too old for that, but it still makes me feel better.

"Can we leave the door open? Just a little bit so that I can see the night-light?"

She pulled me close. Her hair smelled of strawberries. "Whatever you want, hon. I'm just down the hall."

"That's what I want," I replied.

"Okay," she answered, pulling my sheets up and kissing my forehead. "But someday you'll have to get over your fear of the dark."

"It's not the dark I'm afraid of."

"Good night, Charlie," she said, standing in the doorway on her way out.

"Good night," I answered.

I moved to the edge of the bed and looked across the room. The triangle of light from the hall stopped just short of the closet door. Sometimes the closet made light, too, an awful green-brown shade like the water in the creek behind my house where we catch crayfish. It was dark right now.

I felt less scared now because suddenly I was dreaming. First, I dreamed about cowboys and Indians, airplanes and spaceships, baseball and cookies. But soon the dream didn't feel so great.

I was on my bed, floating in the middle of space. I mean, it *felt* like space, but there weren't any stars or planets. Only a lot of dark nothing. I knew I was no longer in my room because I couldn't hear the neighbor's dog barking, and that dog was never quiet. Actually, I couldn't hear anything, not even my own breathing or the rustle of the covers as I crawled to the edge of the bed for a look around.

I felt pricklies on the back of my neck and sat back quickly against the headboard, clutching the pillow in front of me. If I hadn't seen the dark purple of its skin, I wouldn't have known it was coming down at me. Now I wish I hadn't seen it.

It had four sail-shaped wings, swept way back to get me in their folds, like a manta ray I'd seen on the Discovery Channel. Glowing blue feelers dangled down from its stomach like a thousand eyes.

My screams were lost in the darkness as slick, oily skin ate me...

Someone had turned off the light. I didn't know how long I'd slept. At first I thought I was still in the nightmare, but I heard the familiar tick-tock from my Mickey Mouse alarm clock on the nightstand. My sheets and pajamas were wet and smelly with sweat. And all I could think was that someone had turned off the night-light, shut tight the door, and left me here to die. *Shut up!* I told myself. *That's first-grader talk.* I forced myself to shut my eyes tight and try to go to sleep. This time I would not call for Mommy, no matter what I thought I heard.

I was almost asleep when the Bogeyman started making his hungry noises. I think he is part insect 'cause he clicks and slurps and whirs like a giant spider-cricket, or maybe even a roach. I wrapped the pillow around my head and held it tight against my ears. On the wall, I could see the flicky green-brown even with my eyes squeezed tight. I forced myself to not turn around 'cause I knew where that light was coming from; I knew the light was pouring out of the crack around the door.

The light got hotter until my back felt sunburned. Still, I forced myself to stay on this side of the bed and look straight ahead, holding the pillow to my ears, biting my tongue, and blinking out tears from eyes squeezed too tight.

Then the Bogeyman broke the rules. I heard the rusting creak of the closet door hinge.

Impossible. He can't leave the closet!

The creaking got louder, the door almost open...

He was breaking the rules, so what else could I do? And Mom said I was gonna have to face it...someday. Today?

I spun around to face the Bogeyman.

The nightmare was over. I caught my breath. It was just Mom standing there in the open closet.

There was a click and whir when she turned her head to look at me.

"Charlie! What are you doing up? School comes early. You really must get over this foolish fear of the dark!"

I smiled at her and blushed. You'd never think such a baby like me was in third grade!

She smiled lovingly back at me. Then I saw something in her hands. It was round and black, big as a basketball. Its thin, glowing, green arms worked on the mess of wires and motors in her chest. It paused for a second and looked at me with one alien, purple eye. Showing off, it ballooned out its sail-shaped egg sac and slick black wings.

The numbers on the clock clicked over to 9:05.

I screamed and screamed.

ELECTRIC

Ironically, the battle had been fought in the cemetery.

Bodies were scattered among the tombstones, goblins impaled on lances like insects pinned up for examination, alongside knights with raw, smashed-in faces. Only the generals remained to survey the day's carnage.

The dark wizard and the majestic unicorn stood at opposite ends of the field like dueling outlaws under the churning cauldron of gray-black sky. The wizard threw back the hood of his cloak, revealing eyes of green fire. The unicorn bowed his thick mane, his horn pulsating a myriad of colors. The time had come.

A blast of white light shot out from the tip of the unicorn's rainbow horn. The wizard threw his hands in front of his body and yelled an incantation. A blue bubble surrounded the wizard like an egg, and the unicorn's shot bounced off the shield's surface and scorched the earth several yards away from the wizard's position.

The wizard raised his twisted staff and a bolt of lightning erupted from its end. The unicorn leaped gracefully aside, but the shot seared the creature's hindquarters, leaving a dark, jagged scar. The unicorn cried out in anguish, an alien, discordant sound from a voice designed for seraphic melody.

The wizard moved in with confidence, navigating the labyrinth of death-monuments like a spirit. Lightning flew from his staff, shattering the stones that protected the unicorn.

Suddenly a joyful trumpet blast sounded, and Charlie gasped in disbelief as a knight appeared on the right side of the screen. Charlie slammed the joystick to the right, but the wizard turned only in time to meet the point of the knight's lance with his chest. The wizard collapsed, and his body turned to dust as an annoying tune began playing, accompanied by the message, "Once again, good triumphs over evil…"

Finally it ended and the PLAY AGAIN? prompt appeared in the middle of the screen.

Charlie Fielder had always known that he was different, what the other kids called a "nerd" or a "dork." While other boys in grade school had been outside shooting hoops, he had been in front of his ATARI 400, diligently completing his first computer program. In high school he spent the majority of his time studying or playing chess while other kids his age were learning how to French kiss or sneaking into R-rated movies.

Charlie's thoughts were interrupted by the sound of the door swinging open.

"How are things going, Charlie?"

Charlie wheeled around in his chair to face his father. "Fine, Dad. I was just thinking."

His father looked like Ward Cleaver in his plaid pajamas and slippers. "Always glad to hear that, Charlie," said Mr. Fielder, grinning. "Well, good night."

"Good night, Dad." Charlie's father closed the door, and Charlie wheeled back around in his chair to face the computer. The cursor waited patiently at the end of the PLAY AGAIN? prompt.

Charlie flipped the switch on the back of the machine and left the room. Static electricity crackled eerily in the darkness as the fan slowed to a stop.

The second biggest storm that the small town of Pikesville, Pennsylvania, had ever seen unleashed its full fury that night around 2 a.m. Johnny Mills grinned to himself as he sped over the slick asphalt. He smelled of beer and cigarettes.

Johnny wasn't thinking about the storm or about the way the tires of his '74 Dodge Dart slid across the road every so often. He was thinking of Dorene, replaying every moment of their savage coupling up against the back wall of Sam's Bar & Grill, and then the later, the more athletic fusion that occurred in her bedroom. *She was like a gymnast tonight,* thought Johnny, chuckling to himself. *A friggin' gymnast!*

As Johnny turned on to Sweet Creek Road, the rear end of his car swung outward in a controlled skid. Johnny let loose a proud Southern "Yeeeeeehaw!" and pressed down on the accelerator. He was only several minutes from home, and he began to think about his wife. He knew she would be there waiting for him.

Johnny laughed as he envisioned her standing on the porch in curlers and a facial mud pack, perhaps even tapping a large rolling pin against her palm in expectation of his arrival. He was still laughing hysterically when his car slid off of the road.

Charlie had a dream that night. He dreamed of electricity, of traveling through an endless labyrinth of wires that were as large as subway tubes. As he flew through the corridors, he grew stronger. He was being fed like a river with a thousand sources, and each source heightened his malevolence. Each source heightened his need *to kill*.

Charlie knew the entities that fed him. They were scores of squirrels. They were hundreds of birds. And one was a man named Bill McGee. He had been struck by a power line in the Great Storm of '78. All of the creatures that joined Charlie on his wild passage had died by electrocution.

Some, like Bill McGee, had waited nearly thirteen years to free their souls from the TV sets and circuit boxes that had contained them. Finally, another great storm had come.

They were free. And they were *pissed*.

—

Johnny Mills awoke to a horrible blaring noise. At first he thought it was in his head, but then he realized his face was resting on the car horn. He tasted blood on his lips, and his nose throbbed like a primal drumbeat. *Christ,* thought Johnny, *the old lady's going to love this one.*

Johnny climbed out of the car and inspected the damage. The car's front end was crunched in toward the middle, where he had struck the trunk of an oak tree. The headlights were jammed in position, and they peered into the woods like the eyes of a predator. Johnny shook his head in despair and began to climb the steep, grassy embankment toward the road.

Johnny reached the top of the embankment and looked down Sweet Creek Road. A streetlight stood like a lonely sentinel fifty yards down the road. Johnny imagined he could hear the soft hum of the bulb from where he was standing. Something was horribly wrong. He couldn't place it, but it had something to do with the air. The air was charged. It felt as if all of the unseen particles that populated the air around him were in a state of hyperactivity. Then Johnny heard it. A disjointed series of crackling, popping sounds from above.

The last time Johnny had heard something like it was thirteen years ago. His mother was driving him home from soccer practice. He remembered the rain slamming down on to the roof of the car like the fists of God and his throbbing shin that had been kicked by Tommy Nicholson during practice. Flares had been set up on the roadway, and a policeman directed the traffic around a loose wire that snapped and jerked like a viper. Johnny remembered his mother telling him to look away, but it was too late. Several feet away from the officer was a body covered by a raincoat. Johnny remembered thinking that the glistening dress shoes that stuck out from under the coat were polished and the darkest black he had ever seen.

A distinctive *crack!* pulled Johnny out of the memory. He spun his head upward as a wire broke free from a nearby telephone pole. He knew he had to run: the images of the dead man under the raincoat were still hotly pressed into his consciousness, but he was frozen in place by what he saw at the wire's end as it swung down toward him. First it was a squirrel's head with pulsating red eyes. Then it was the stark, velvet face of a crow ringed in phosphorescent fire. Then he saw the face of a middle-aged man with thinning hair and vibrant green eyes. As the wire fell, the shapes changed and merged with such dizzying speed that Johnny could no longer make out the individual forms, just a collage of images that resembled a primal, demonic mask. Johnny thought it was the most beautiful thing he had ever seen. Finally it all disappeared, replaced by the sinister face of Charlie Fielder.

The wire struck Johnny and seemed to hold him there as the forms fell upon him in a feeding frenzy. Johnny's face instantly lost its dreamy countenance and was twisted into a never-ending scream as his soul was drawn from his body. Streams of blood shot out of his nose and mouth. Several seconds later, his eyeballs popped out of their sockets and landed with a *plop! plop!* in the spreading puddle of blood on the glazed pavement.

After several moments, the forms released Johnny and shrieked off into the mantled heavens. Johnny's body rolled heavily down the embankment like a sack of potatoes. At last it was still, and the empty sockets stared into the blazing glare of the Dart's headlights.

Charlie was awakened by a crashing peal of thunder. His pajamas were damp with perspiration and his mouth felt like it was stuffed full of cotton. His heart was racing as he reached over and turned on the lamp.

That was one hell of a dream, thought Charlie as he rubbed his eyes and groped for his glasses on the nightstand. His clock radio read 3:30 a.m. in large red digits.

Charlie rose out of bed groggily and started toward the kitchen. The thunder crashed again and shook the entire house as he navigated the dark hallway. He descended the staircase feeling drained and dizzy, as if he might lose his balance at any moment. He held on to the railing at the bottom for several moments before he continued his odyssey toward the kitchen.

Charlie froze. Someone was standing by the French doors. He crept forward, his feet silent on the thick shag carpet. The lightning flashed, revealing the face of a man who had weathered his share of life's miseries. It was his father's face, but its grim countenance seemed to belong to a stranger.

"Dad?" asked Charlie hesitantly.

"Oh, hello, son. Storm keeping you up?" Mr. Fielder smiled warmly, and Charlie immediately began to feel a little better.

"No, I had a nightmare. I thought I would get some milk to help me sleep."

"Well, get your milk and keep an old man company."

Charlie forced a smile. *Old. That had been exactly how his father had looked.*

Charlie walked into the kitchen, and his father turned his attention back to the storm. As Charlie began to pour the milk, his father started speaking in the next room. His voice was as slow and deliberate as rain. "Haven't had a storm like this in over ten years, Charlie. Not since you were struck by lightning."

Charlie almost dropped his glass as he walked out of the kitchen. His father was no longer standing and had settled into his favorite easy chair. Charlie sat down on the couch. He felt dizzy again, and his throat scratched like sandpaper. He drank the milk greedily, spilling some of it down the front of his shirt.

"Easy, son, we don't want it coming back up," his father said jokingly.

Charlie licked his lips before speaking. "Did you say I was struck by lightning, Dad?"

"Yes, I did. It was one of the strangest things I've ever seen. It happened when you were four years old. You were with your mother, and I was in the kitchen while we were fixing dinner. A storm was coming, just as the meteorologist had predicted, and the wind had picked up outside so that you could hear it rushing through the trees. The lightning was what really caught your eye, Charlie. You were staring at it like it was Christ himself. Your mother and I didn't think too much of it, you being a kid and all. Well, the next time we turned around, you were gone. We rushed to the back door and saw you walking through the fields. We ran outside and hollered your name, but you just kept on walking. Then you were struck."

Charlie's father paused and looked at Charlie, who was shaking all over.

"Like I said, it was eerie, like something out of a horror movie. You actually glowed, Charlie, and your hair stood straight up in the air. The lightning didn't strike you and disappear; it stayed right on you, changing from blue to white and then back to blue again as if it were feeding you. Your mother and I were running toward you, and she was screaming, 'Charlie's dead! My Charlie's dead!'

"The lightning disappeared before we reached you, and you just stood there as still as an oak. I thought you had died standing up. When we reached you, you couldn't move or speak. We carried you into the house and called an ambulance, but by the time it arrived, you were acting normally. We had the paramedics check you out just in case, but they decided that you were perfectly healthy. We didn't see any reason for you to go to the hospital, and that was the end of it. You never did remember getting struck, though."

"Why didn't you tell me this before, Dad?"

A hardness washed across the face of Charlie's dad. The thunder crashed, and he slowly turned his face toward the small windowpanes in the French doors. Charlie thought he looked like a stranger again.

"I lost my best friend that night, Charlie," said Mr. Fielder in a hoarse whisper as his eyes searched for something in the night. "His name was Bill McGee. He was struck by a loose power line. I hope you can understand why I wouldn't want to talk about it. Son, are you alright? You look as pale as a ghost."

"Yeah, just a little tired," Charlie said softly. He looked out into the rural darkness and thought he saw a child walking through the fields. "Can we continue this talk tomorrow, Dad?"

"Sure thing, Charlie. Sure thing. Don't forget to turn the kitchen light out, okay?"

Charlie noticed the semi-dry streaks of tears on his father's face as his father leaned over to pat his knee. "I won't. Good night." He watched his father's slippered feet shuffle down the hallway until they turned the corner, and then Charlie realized he was still in a state of shock.

Parts of the dream were coming back to Charlie, parts that he hadn't remembered upon waking. These were images of him rising out of bed and walking zombie-like toward the study, turning on the computer and doing something…something unnatural with his hands. The images came clearly without the hazy distortion so characteristic of dreams.

Charlie rose. Fear trickled down his spine like ice-cold water. Voices nagged his brain like an angry jury as he walked silently down the hall: *Was it a dream, Charlie? Or did something happen with you and that computer? Some kind of horrible interface of man and machine that transformed you from Charlie Fielder to Charles Manson?*

Charlie reached the door of the study. Faint bluish light spilled out of the crack beneath the doorway like radiation. Charlie pushed the door open.

The light was coming from the monitor. A high-resolution image of Sweet Creek Road stared at Charlie like a silicon nightmare. There were skid marks on the asphalt, and a downed power line swung in the wind like a dead limb. As Charlie advanced toward the monitor, the image rotated. Now Charlie faced the shoulder of the road where the skid marks met the grass. He now knew something horrible lay at the bottom of the embankment, something the voices in his head already knew about.

Perspiration beaded Charlie's face as he paused in the darkness. The voices came on strong, yelling accusations of cowardice. Finally, he managed to put one foot in front of the other and continue to the computer.

The picture on the monitor scrolled down the embankment as Charlie drew closer to the computer. Johnny Mill's Dodge Dart came into view, looking like a wounded dinosaur as its headlights peered into the heart of the woods. Charlie approached the computer, and the picture zoomed in on the corpse of Johnny Mills. His pale, eyeless face looked like the face of a plastic mannequin smeared in red paint.

Charlie reached out to touch the screen, and the picture began to break up. In several seconds the screen was blank and the green characters P-L-A-Y AG-A-I-N-? took form within the inky background. The blinking cursor flashed at the end of the message, awaiting his response with the regularity of a heartbeat.

Charlie felt an intense, throbbing warmth in his fingertips. A soft, fleshy glow drummed beneath the skin of each fingertip in the rhythm of the cursor. The keys on the keyboard had melted together so that the letters were stretched and disfigured like a schizophrenic's alphabet soup. Two handprints were molded into the melted plastic.

Charlie sat down in front of the computer and eased his hands into the molds on the keyboard. His face was no longer the face of a docile, pimply teenager. It was the face of a barbarian just before the slaughter. The PLAY AGAIN? prompt was replaced by a long, circular tunnel. Blue strands of electricity shot out of the keyboard and tied Charlie's hands down in a pulsating web. No knight was going to appear on the right side of the screen now.

This time Charlie was playing to win.

CLUB MITTERNACHT

Dave Morris's eyes bristled with excitement as he walked into Club Mitternacht. A gray film of smoke hovered over the bar area, dimming the pink neon pulsations of a Becks beer sign. An old geezer teetered on his stool, grinning slyly at a young woman at the bar. She sucked on a Marlboro and blew smoke signals in his direction that read "piss off." The bartender leaned against the bar, his eyes staring into the haze as he toyed with his wristwatch.

Dave's eyes lost their fevered brilliance. *Damn,* he thought, *just another dive bar.*

Dave had come to Club Mitternacht looking for deviants. He had an interest in all things off of the beaten path: cemeteries, punk rock, poetry, gothic architecture... you name it. If it was something that most people considered strange, Dave was into it.

Not that he had consciously decided to be weird; these just happened to be the things that inspired him to write, and anybody who knew Dave knew he was, first and foremost, a writer. He knew inspiration when it showed its shy face, and he grabbed it whenever it came around, weird or not.

Now the only thing Dave could think about was the four marks he had apparently wasted to get into Club Mitternacht. *It had seemed to hold so much promise!* Tucked away neatly into a cobblestone lane, Club Mitternacht looked like the perfect haven for deviants who longed to get out of the cold, gray climate of Northern Germany. *How disappointing.*

Vibrations traveled up through the soles of Dave's feet and rocked his whole frame. Somebody was playing music downstairs. Its tempo was frightening; it cranked out of the speakers like dust devils. Dave approached the bar. The bartender instantly became animated, anxious to do anything but sit and wait.

Dave looked down at his Levi's and T-shirt. One hundred percent Americano.

"*Guten abend,*" Dave said. "*Ich mochte ein* Becks *Bier, bitte.*"

The bartender gave him a "You're not from around here, are you?" look and reached under the counter. Out of the corner of his eye, Dave thought he saw a dark shape slink through a doorway near the end of the bar.

The bartender placed a cool green bottle of Becks on a Club Mitternacht coaster and pushed it toward Dave.

"*Vier mark, bitte.*"

"*Ja,*" Dave said as he fished in his pockets for change, "*ein moment.*"

He found the money but held it in his hands to keep the bartender's attention.

"*Wissen sie was ist...*" The bartender looked at Dave expectantly. *Shit,* thought Dave, *what's the word for "downstairs"?* He could only remember the word for "under."

It would have to do.

"*Was ist unter?*" he asked, pointing downward and feeling a bit foolish.

"*Du kannst* English *sprechen,*" laughed the bartender.

"Okay...thanks." Dave let a sigh of relief escape his lips. "I was wondering what's going on downstairs."

"Through there?" asked the bartender pointing to the smoke-shrouded doorway descending into the darkness.

Dave nodded.

"The punks are down there. The punks and that noise and that damn rainbow."

"That what?"

"The rainbow. It's a...how do you say...lightwork?"

"Lightshow!" quipped Dave.

"Yes, that's it. But perhaps it is better that you drink up here at the bar. I don't trust those punks. You shouldn't either."

"Thanks for the beer," said Dave, handing the bartender a pair of two-mark coins. Then he turned and headed straight for the stairs.

"*Viel gluck,*" the bartender muttered under his breath.

———

Dave took the worn, slick, wooden steps two at a time. He couldn't wait to meet the noisemakers downstairs. His leap off of the last step seemed like a leap out of reality and into another world.

Music thumped through the place: desperate and primal, filled with shrill caterwauls and velveteen hisses. A striking couple of punkers were seated in the center of the room. The male had sharp, hawklike features and a bleached shock of hair that contrasted sharply with his black leather jacket and pants. The female sat opposite the male. Long onyx hair streaked with silver spilled down her back. A studded belt held her biker jacket closed at the waist. She wore no shirt underneath, and the exposed V-neck of flesh glistened with a gray sheen. A shower of prismatic tones had been projected onto the far wall by projectors suspended from the ceiling. Beams of light radiated out from a pinpoint center and swirled around the wall, going from dimness to brilliance in a matter of seconds. A ghoulish-looking punker in the DJ booth controlled the projectors as they swiveled around madly, his deft hands hovering over the control board and making lightning-quick adjustments. Strands of dry ice rose off of the empty dance floor. The small modernistic tables were arranged in curved lines that radiated out from the table in the center of the room where the striking couple was seated.

Dave let out an inaudible gasp. *It's all so...so religious,* he thought. He had never felt more like an outsider.

Some of the tables were occupied by other leather-clad teenagers. Dave noticed that nobody was smoking or drinking. No one was dancing. All were absorbed in the whirling prismatic projection on the far wall.

The female punker with streaked hair swiped at her male counterpart to get his attention. They both turned to regard Dave. Seconds passed as the beat droned on. Finally the girl motioned Dave over. A slender punker carried over an extra stool to their table.

Eyes bored into Dave's back as he walked toward the table. His mouth went dry and his hands began to shake. The bottom of his stomach fell out like a trapdoor; for a moment he thought he was going to vomit.

The punker with the bleached hair noticed Dave's discomfort. He looked at the others and hissed sharply. The gawkers turned back to the light show.

"You mussst excussse my friendsss," he said as Dave climbed onto the stool.

"We don't sssee many new people come in here. Essspecially Americansss." His words slipped and slid like tires not quite catching wet pavement.

"Your English is quite good," said Dave, trying to keep a straight face. *Yeah,* he thought, *except for the fact that you speak like a snake.*

"My name is Ssspin. Thisss isss Reflex," he said, introducing himself and the girl with the black, black hair.

Dave turned to the rainbow to keep from laughing. *Spin and Reflex. Jesus.*

"Incredible light show," said Dave.

"The rainbow? Nothing more than a pretty focal point, really. We can thank Felix for itsss hypnotic effect," said Spin, pointing to the mohawked punker in the DJ booth.

"A focal point? What are you trying to focus?" Dave asked, perplexed.

"Our thoughtsss, of courssse," replied the girl. "It'sss like the crystalsss of the New Agersss. Except that all of usss focusss our energy on the rainbow. Asss a group, we can do the mossst amazing thingsss with our mindsss."

Spin kicked Reflex under the table before she could continue.

"Reflex," said Spin slyly, "look at Katerina. Ssshe ssseemsss to be taking an interessst in our American friend."

Dave turned around and followed Spin's gaze. The most beautiful girl he had ever seen was smiling widely at him, the colors of the rainbow reflecting eerily off of her small, unblemished teeth. Two forest-green eyes penetrated the bangs that fell over her forehead and caught Dave like hooks.

"Ssshe wantsss to dance," hissed Spin. "Go to her."

Dave stepped off of his stool and began to move toward the girl. She stepped down to greet him, her taut feminine frame rippling beneath her black tights.

Katerina took Dave by the hand and led him to the dance floor. Felix grinned as they passed the DJ booth. His hands danced over to the control board on his right. The tiles of the dance floor began to glow beneath the temporal mist provided by the dry ice machine.

Katerina began to circle Dave in small prancing steps, her hands caressing him with serpentine fluidity. The beat pumped furiously onward as Felix's hands soared over the controls. The shrill caterwauls and stiletto hisses rose in a tempest of sound. Katerina's movements became wild, desperate.

Then it all stopped. The only sound was the slow, unified breath of the punkers. Dave felt detached, hypnotized; it was as if everything was taking place on film.

BOOM-BOOM. Two bass tones sounded in rapid succession. Dave blinked as the cameras, now fixed in position like metallic bats, fired simultaneously with the primal beat.

BOOM-BOOM. FLASH-FLASH.

BOOM-BOOM. FLASH-FLASH.

Katerina thrust herself against Dave. She was warm and supple, and her coupled, synchronized thrusts fired him. The chanting began, a hiss like rushing air.

"Is-sa! Is-sa!"

BOOM-BOOM. FLASH-FLASH.

Katerina began to kiss Dave methodically with her full, perfect lips. Occasionally her pink tongue darted out between her even teeth to lick his face. Dave's eyes were half-closed in pleasure, and in the misty darkness he imagined Katerina's eyes had assumed a saturnine aspect.

"Is-sa! Is-sa!"

Katerina pushed her full body against him. They kissed violently on the mouth, oblivious to the ritual around them. Her hands dug into Dave's back, and he felt a tinge of pain as Katerina's fingers moved down toward his waist.

"Is-sa! Is-sa!"

An intoxicating warmth spread outwards from Dave's back and filled him with silken comfort. He felt a rumbling beneath his feet. With tremendous effort he managed to raise the lead curtains that were his eyelids.

The section of the dance floor in front of the rainbow had separated and moved apart. Rising out of the floor was a rough block of stone covered with hieroglyphics.

Dave's eyelids began to slowly fall downward. All of the punkers were on the dance floor and whirling about him, playfully inflicting shallow scratches on his exposed arms and face.

Spin and Reflex moved in close, grinning demonically. They had changed.

Their faces were completely covered in fur, and their wide yellow-green eyes rested above a pink triangle of a nose. Hisses rushed out of their mouths between their small, perfect teeth like wind.

Dave's eyelids were falling. With Herculean effort, he managed to slow the process. But sleep was inevitable. The feline faces that swirled around him made him dizzy.

Through the slits of his vision Dave saw something flicker on top of the ancient carved stone. Finally, it achieved substance.

A huge black cat now sat on the stone. It moved its head slowly back and forth like a queen surveying her court. An amber gem around its neck pulsed in time to the feverish chant.

"Is-sa," Dave muttered as his eyelids finally fell shut.

The sky was gray in Northern Germany. A scrap of paper fumbled its way down a narrow cobblestone street and was swept upward into the cold neon tubing that formed the words "Club Mitternacht." In the alley behind the club, a pack of stray cats slowly moved toward the street in a rag-tag convoy. They were led by a brown cat with a bleach-blonde stripe down its back and a slender black cat with silver streaks running from its eyes to the back of its head. The rear of the march was brought up by an awkward-moving calico.

The convoy moved forward from the alley and turned onto the street.

The clumsy calico stopped and looked down the alley that ran alongside Club Mitternacht. Its face was covered with scratches.

"Isssa," it hissed, then turned and ran to catch up with the rest of the pack.

THE WITCH TOASTER

Of course, they were all too terrified to talk about it. The witch had only been fired three days before, and management tended to make these changes in batches lately.

When George Reiner saw Renee Summers in the kitchen, they were confronted by Audrey's toaster and could no longer avoid the topic.

"Do you think we should take it back or something?" Renee asked.

"Do you want to take it back?" George mocked.

"Thanks but no thanks—I'd rather not come back as a toad!"

As they were laughing, a young programmer named Chao walked in and grabbed his lunch out of the fridge. He pulled out two slices of bread from his bag and made his way toward the toaster.

George watched him in shock. "You can't be serious!" blurted Renee.

Chao shrugged. "Why not? The crazy girl is gone, isn't she?" Without further debate, Chao dropped his bread into the slots and pulled down the lever to start the toasting process. There was some crackling and popping as the toaster warmed up.

"Piece of junk," Chao said, disgusted. Renee and George just looked on.

After about a minute the toaster began to shake and sputter green puffs of smoke. George sprang into action, snatching the plug out of the socket and causing small golden sparks to fly.

"My toast!" protested Chao.

A minute later, the toast popped up, blackened on the edges.

They all gazed silently as Chao withdrew the toast from the toaster. Each slice had been branded with a pentagram.

Paul Sweeney was nothing if not prompt. He called the staff meeting to order sharply at 8:30 a.m.

"As you all know, Audrey Morningrose was let go on Friday. There are rumors circulating around the office that Audrey was released due to her religion."

"You mean witchcraft," corrected Kamir.

"No, Kamir, that is not what I mean," Mr. Sweeney replied sternly. "As she stated, Audrey practiced Wicca, a religion officially recognized by the federal government. She was not—I repeat was *not*—released because of her religion." Mr. Sweeney looked around at each of his staff members in turn for effect.

"She was probably fired for not sobbing his knob," Renee whispered to George.

George twisted his face to suppress a grin.

"Is there something else you'd like to add, Ms. Summers?"

"Er, uh, I said she was probably fired because she didn't like kabobs."

Mr. Sweeney gave Renee an odd look. "Uh, no, not that either. Audrey's release was purely performance-related. Speaking of that, I'd say it's time we all get back to it. Meeting adjourned."

After the clicking shut of laptop lids and a rustle of papers being hurriedly gathered, the conference room once again went silent.

—

The staff had gathered in George Reiner's cube to conspire.

"So what if everything Audrey left behind was cursed?" Renee asked.

"Let's not get ahead of ourselves. We don't know that anything was cursed," George asserted. "Maybe the toaster just malfunctioned."

"Malfunctioned. Yes. We all know the power is really bad here," Chao concurred.

"C'mon guys. A malfunction that specifically burns pentagrams into bread? Sweeney can call it Wicca or whatever, but as Kamir said, Audrey was a straight-up witch, and I don't mean the good kind. You remember her raving about those parties she had with her coven. They sounded like orgies to me."

"Yes, listen to Renee, system analysts are very practical," Kamir added.

"George," Renee asked in a seductive tone, placing a hand on George's shoulder, "do that thing with your account. Let's see what Renee was up to before she left."

"No. Absolutely not. 'That thing with my account,' as you put it, could get me fired."

"Do it! Do it! Do it!" the small group chanted. They had used this technique on George frequently in the past to get him to use his special back door into other systems, and to date, it had never failed them.

George held up his hands in protest. "Alright, alright, I'll do it! Just give me some space here."

The group backed up as much as possible in the cramped cubicle to watch George work his magic.

He clicked on the picture of his cocker spaniel, Ruthie, and a black window appeared on the computer's desktop with a flashing green command prompt. He began to type in strange commands using numerous special characters as his audience murmured in amazement.

"Like Master Yoda," whispered Kamir to the others.

Suddenly the window filled with another computer's desktop, its normal icons replaced by Celtic runes.

"That's Audrey's for sure," remarked Renee.

"Thank you, Renee, for pointing out the obvious. Now, where to?"

"There," uttered Chao in a somber tone, and the others watched in horror as his trembling finger pointed to an icon labeled *Dark Secrets*.

Without hesitation, George clicked on the icon.

For a moment nothing happened, and then suddenly the screen went totally black as swirls of purples, pinks, and oranges filled the void like a space nebula.

The colors then gathered and reformed, becoming the outline of a face.

"It's her!" exclaimed Kamir, and indeed, it was Audrey's countenance staring back and them.

Then the face pressed forward, causing the screen to melt like liquid as Audrey's face probed outward. George was mesmerized, frozen in his chair. Just before the angry, flaring nose of Audrey connected with his own, George shrieked and jumped back.

Sparks flew from the wall, CPU, and monitor all at once.

Then it was over, leaving the smell of burned plastic in the air that made the group want to gag.

"Oh my God, George! When did you last back up your code?" asked Kamir.

"Friday. Audrey's last day."

"Cursed," whispered Kamir.

Like magic, they all received black envelopes the next day. There was no doubt where they came from. The alternating skull and dagger pattern could only be Audrey's mark.

The envelope contained a single page of black parchment adorned in ornate crimson calligraphy: *Beware Paul. He has targeted all of you.*

This time, they had no choice. An offsite lunch was mandatory.

Union Station was a bustling place. In addition to numerous eateries and shops, it was also the hub for both Amtrak commuter trains and the Metro. The team sat at a table in Sbarro, talking excitedly and sharing pizza and pasta.

"I'm a bit concerned about all of this. Do you guys think we should tell corporate about this?" asked Renee.

"Are you crazy? We have stumbled upon an ancient power from the gods, and you want to give it to the Man!" blurted Kamir.

George scoffed between bites of a calzone. "Kamir, you grew up in India. How do you even know about the Man?"

"The movies. I just watched *Boyz in the Hood*," Kamir asserted.

George shook his head.

"Maybe Kamir is right," stated Chao. "If Audrey is warning us, we should listen."

Renee nodded. "I see your point, guys. I would trust Audrey before Paul Sweeney."

"Okay, Ms. Analyst, then what do we do?" asked George.

Renee paused for a nanosecond to think. "Well, let's treat it like a computer bug. First, we need to collect more data to reproduce the issue."

The team looked back at her, puzzled, collectively gulping down soda.

"All I mean is this: We know what the toaster can do. We know that the computer is straight-up possessed. Let's see what we can learn from the rest of Audrey's stuff. Unless, of course, you numb-nuts have a better idea?" She was glowing with girl power.

The guys looked at each other nervously.

Finally Kamir spoke. "I think we don't."

———

The Hewlett Packard OfficeJet 6110 printer did not stand a chance.

The five of them glared down at the device menacingly as they stood in a half circle in Audrey's old cube.

"I feel almost bad for it," whispered Kamir. "It seems so helpless."

"Grow a pair, Kamir! It's a goddamn printer," fumed Renee.

After another moment of inaction by the men, Renee grabbed a piece of paper, placed the page in the feeder, and hit the copy button. The printer's clicking and whirring was expected, even comforting, but the strange green glow was not. Finally, the printer was silent. No paper came back out from either return.

"Typical," muttered Chao, "the page jammed."

George shook his head. "No, I don't think so. The error light is not flashing."

"I have an idea," Renee blurted. She grabbed the heavy-duty black stapler, placed it on the flatbed scanning area of the printer, and hit the button. The rest of the group looked puzzled. With a click and a whir, another blast of eerie green light, and just like that, the stapler was gone.

The group let out a collective gasp.

"Holy cow!" exclaimed Kamir. "It's gone!"

"Not completely. Look!" pointed Renee. A slender black "V," a two-dimensional rendition of the stapler, came out of the printer.

Before they could reflect any further, Paul Sweeney pushed his way into the circle.

"What the hell is going on here? Why aren't you working?" His beady eyes looked as though they would burst out of his head.

There are some moments in life when you simply react without thinking, like in combat. For George Zimmer, this was one of those moments. He grabbed Paul by his artsy tie and dragged his head and neck toward the printer. The printer hungrily hummed to life, a green cloud in the form of Audrey's face surging forward to claim the sacrifice.

"Help me!" George exclaimed, wrestling to get Paul's ample legs and torso forward. George's grasp of Paul's tie was so tight that purple veins protruded from Paul's forehead as he struggled to breathe.

Finally, the group managed to get Paul in front of the printer. From there, Audrey did the rest. First, his head shrunk to the size of a pinhead, and then his shoulders became little more than a roll of onion skin. Although Paul no longer offered any resistance, the group kept pushing him forward, months and years of repressed anger feeding them just as they fed Paul to the unholy witch light. They were in a sort of frenzy, a mass hysteria, as they collectively committed murder.

Finally, it was done, and they huddled together, panting.

"He's gone," stated Kamir somberly.

"Not completely . . . look!" said Renee in a hushed whisper.

A slender silhouette was coming out of the printer, no thicker than a gingerbread man.

After that day, things were different in the Information Technology Department. Always there was soft New Age music playing in the background, and the chitchat of pleasant conversation, punctuated at times by laughter. When visitors came to the department, they were overcome with a feeling of well-being and positivity. Productivity was up, and management was happy. In short, life was good.

Life was good for George Reiner as well. He had been promoted to Department Manager, and he had a new bounce in his step as he made his way through the carpeted hallways. This was not only due to his recent promotion. Several months after "the event" with Paul Sweeney (for this was how they always referred to it), he had proposed to Renee, and she had accepted.

A silhouette of a man was taped to the wall of George's cube, and sometimes, in the early morning before the murmur and rhythms of work swung into full gear, small pitiful sounds issued from its tiny mouth when the tape they'd placed there eventually fell off.

But they had plenty of tape, and this, too, would pass in good time. Should the witch have her old job back?

THE LAND SPIDER

The old Indians were looking at the hole again. I studied the familiar scene with disbelief. I had tried to tell them there was nothing supernatural about a sinkhole; sometimes the earth just isn't set right and it gives way. But they continued their talk of a great spider that spun out these mesas and canyons as easily as silk. I remember telling them that any creature living under New Mexico would have been scared up by the nuclear testing at White Sands.

That hadn't gone over too well.

So day after day, they come to worship at the hole, bringing their exotic paints and prayer sticks, their vibrant masks and headdresses, dancing their wild dances and preaching their stories of gloom and doom.

All of this should give me something to write about. I haven't had a legitimate inspiration since holing up in this dustbin of a town.

It's not that I regret leaving the University of New Mexico. They could take their criticisms and stick 'em where the sun doesn't shine. I know I'm good. I only wish my typewriter would agree with me.

Finally the old Indians moved on, making signs of protection against the eight evil eyes of the spider, which they thought was waiting for them in the bowels of the earth. I was glad to see them go. They made me nervous.

Outside, the night was approaching. Nights in New Mexico aren't like nights anywhere else. You feel the night as it falls down on the desert. The sky weighs on your shoulders like a sack of bright blue stones: cold, heavy night presses. Watching the nightfall from the east to the west gives me the creeps.

The hole across the street loses its well-defined edges and chalky appeal and becomes a formless, dark maw.

Somewhere down there in that void is Sam's Service Station.

I was sitting at my desk when it happened last month, scanning the blue expanse for inspiration for my novel.

I had never seen anything like it. The earth opened up right before my eyes, and the station just gave way like it was made of Lincoln Logs. I remember Sam Harold's face as it happened, his mouth stretched wide in wonder, his eyes sparkling with adrenaline as he gripped the doorframe. Sometimes in the middle of the night I think I hear him moving around down there, sifting around through the dirt in his grease-covered T-shirt, asking over and over again with hollow eyes and a thin voice like the breeze across the desert, "Fill 'er up, Mike? Fill 'er up?"

A wind swept across the road and kicked up dust, stirring me from my dark reverie. I moved away from the window and opened up the paperback on my nightstand, trying to think about anything besides the hole and Sam Harold's screaming face sinking into the ground.

Around ten o'clock, I went down to the bar. I had grown tired of sitting in front of my typewriter, trying to concentrate on that clear field of white paper that stared back at me and begged for some embellishment.

Ideas had fluttered before my mind's eye like troublesome moths, then scattered away with the speed of dragonflies as I reached out to grab them.

Underlying it all was the hole across the street, that pool of black which made me look out the window from time to time and which kept my heart thrumming in my chest.

As I entered the bar I spied Joe filling a pitcher of beer. Of course I knew his real name wasn't Joe. Who ever heard of an Indian named Joe? But he protected his Indian name, said it was a gift which had only been earned by his wife. Same old sacred bullshit.

Joe threw a look in my direction, nodded, and then turned back to the tap. Joe was young but had the look of one who knows the way of things. His grandfather had given him the bar and the rooms above it before he died, but Joe had not assumed his grandfather's ceremonial role in the shrinking tribe.

Joe strode over to me. "The usual, Mike?" he asked slyly, his granite features breaking into a wide grin. Joe said he had his grandfather's looks. His grandfather must have been a hard-looking man.

"Yeah, the usual," I replied, grinning back.

Joe popped the cap off of a Corona and placed it on a coaster in front of me. I noticed that several of the elders who were at the hole earlier were talking excitedly in the corner, gesturing in sweeping motions, the meaning of which escaped me.

Joe followed my gaze. "They're getting ready, Mike. Telling the tales of their youth to prepare for their deaths."

"Deaths? You can't possibly be talking about that thing underground?"

"Not *thing*, Mike. Spider. God."

"Okay, I'll humor you for a moment. Assuming that this thing is going to suck everybody underground the way Sam Harold and his service station went, what makes you people hang around? Why not bug out?"

Joe smiled the smile that wise men give to the ignorant. "You do not understand, Mike. There is no place to go. If the spider draws in her web, she will take everything with it. We'll go first because she chooses to live here in Salt Flat. It is hallowed ground in that sense. But even the towns of your people will eventually be pulled down. It's all part of her web. But here we're at the center. We'll go first."

A slight tremor shook the bar, making the glasses on the shelves strike one another with the sound of wind chimes. The bar went silent, and the old Indians stared ahead with patient, calm eyes. It passed as quickly as it had come.

Joe stared back at me, all granite this time.

"Prepare yourself," he said sternly, and walked to the other side of the bar to pray with the other Indians.

I decided to have my beer in my room.

Once alone again in my room, my unease returned, and I had to pull the shades down to regain my composure. I had removed my private stock of Jack Daniels from my dresser and felt much better after a couple of shots.

Around midnight I drifted off to sleep, having produced nothing more on the page than an ominous title: "The Land Spider."

The dream actually started quite nicely. I was strolling through the desert vigorously, inspired by the mystery of the night and the vast emptiness that is New Mexico. As I approached the town, I noticed a dark well on its fringe, and recognized it by its proximity to the bar as the sinkhole which had swallowed Sam's service station. Suddenly, I was startled by loud, muffled sounds like subterranean explosions. The whole landscape seemed to rock with each beat of that horrible drum, tilting on its side as if seen from an oblique angle. I watched in horror as two hairy legs reached upward from the lip of the sinkhole and caught hold on the sandy earth. I wanted to run back into the night, back toward the desert and its hollow embrace. But I was frozen.

Two more legs emerged from the void and latched onto the earth.

Then it pulled itself forth.

It was a horrible tarantula thing. But it had Sam's face. It was looking at me with the same look Joe had given me after the tremor in the bar and repeating over and over again in a liquid, raspy voice like a broken reed: "Prepare yourself, prepare yourself, prepare…"

Shouts outside my window woke me with a start.

The sun was sitting in the middle of the sky, making me shield my heavy-lidded eyes. I stumbled toward the window. A large crowd had gathered toward the end of the main strip, dancing, gesturing, and kneeling before a large hole in the earth where the general store used to be.

I quickly threw on some jeans and ran down the street toward the crowd. Joe was there, kneeling in the dirt and adding brilliant, crimson grains of sand to a sand painting by the lip of the hole. As I drew closer, I noticed that Joe was adding the fire-red specks to the depiction of a black widow. He looked up, hearing my approach.

"It won't be long now," he said in a flat tone, looking beyond me. "The general store went down very quickly, like a flash of lightning. Nobody even saw it go. She's getting stronger, Mike. Are you ready?"

Something in the way Joe looked terrified me. It was like the look on Sam Harold's face as he went down with the service station. It was the look of someone who knew they were about to die. Joe looked away from me toward some invisible point in the distance.

Then he threw himself into the hole.

I slowly stepped away from the pit, then turned and sprinted toward the bar. The tremors had started again, and the earth seemed to creak and groan like the timbers of an old ship being ripped apart on the rocks.

I knew Joe had been right. There wasn't much time. Enough to get the car keys, maybe enough to pull the plug out of the wall and snatch the typewriter.

She could have the rest.

The tremors were getting very serious, and plaster dust blinded my eyes as I grabbed the typewriter and the car keys. I looked back into the room that had witnessed my soul-searching and neuroses for the last month, feeling a strange twang of remorse. I took a swig of Jack Daniels for good luck and left the rest, taking the stairs two at a time on my way out.

As I ran across the road visions of bad horror films filled my head, images of cars which never started when danger was at hand. The non-Indian members of the town were running about in pure panic, like ants whose hill had just been leveled by a lawn mower.

The Indians held their ground. I watched in horror as the bank was swallowed up. I threw open the door of my Escort and threw my Smith-Corona carelessly onto the passenger seat. The engine turned over easily, and I shifted into gear and took off down the street, honking my horn and swerving to miss the crazed populace. At the edge of town, a Spanish woman was chasing a group of chickens across the road. Her face was covered in blood from a blow to the head, and she had the dazed, shell-shocked look of someone whose house was just bombed. I tore over the chickens, trying to block out the sickening crunch of their bones as they were run down. In my rearview mirror, I saw several buildings go down simultaneously in clouds of dust. I thought of old pictures I had seen of the smoking warships in Pearl Harbor before they had made their final journey to the bottom of the harbor.

The ground beneath me opened up like a trap door.

The car and a chunk of land about ten yards in diameter began to slide slowly backward into the earth. I hit the brakes, screamed and pounded on the wheel, started to rip off my seat belt but then realized there was no place to go, no way to get out. I was being pulled deeper and deeper, but the movement was very smooth as if I were on a cable car being pulled down a mountainside. I watched with morbid fascination as I descended. It seemed as if the whole world was being sucked down into this cavern.

Sunlight streamed down through the enormous gaps in the earth as if threading its way through the trees in a dense forest. Everywhere I looked, stretches of land were being pulled down toward the earth's center, pulled toward *her*. Some of the living were in a state of panic, walking around on their little islands with the same look of bewilderment that had marked the face of the woman chasing the chickens. Others just sat and cried.

An old Indian from the town passed me overhead.

I shouted, but he paid no heed. He sat with his legs crossed and looked serenely down into the darkness.

His gaze seemed to mock me with its indifference.

Joe's voice came back to me: *Are you ready? Not thing, Mike. Spider. God. Hallowed ground. Everything will go. Are you ready?*

I sang, I cried, I prayed every prayer I knew. I told everybody I loved them, that I was sorry if I ever hurt them, ever screwed them, ever let them down. I danced to old rock 'n' roll songs in my head. I remembered the taste of hot chocolate and Coca-Cola. I remembered swimming in the ocean and getting busted for smoking pot on the beach. I remembered my first fight, my first lay. Finally, I remembered to thank Joe for showing me the way.

I sat on the earth in a lotus position, drained and exhausted. I was descending, descending, far beyond the reach of sunlight, ready to mix my blood with the soil, ready to become food for a god.

HARLEY'S CASE

No, it hasn't stopped raining. I imagine it will continue into the night. Can I get you another drink? No? Well, I'll fix myself another. I've been a complete wreck since Harley's death. Haven't slept in days. Not a wink. I know what people are saying; they feel I am somehow responsible for Harley's death. As if I could have stopped it! Fools!

    Fifty men could not have saved Harley from his fate. Harley was tinkering with the natural order of things, forces that tolerate temporary distortion but which ultimately unfailingly return to equilibrium. And then there's the creature. Harley didn't know when to stop pulling its tail. That's a rather poor analogy, I suppose. The creature had no tail.

    But I get ahead of myself. Let me start at the beginning.

    Several weeks ago, a strange thing began happening to me. Just before slipping off into sleep, I would fall into some sort of trance. Low, resonant sounds echoed within my head as if it were an empty cavern. Then I began to see blurry shapes moving around, like figures within smoke or mist. After several moments in this horrific state, another sound joined the chorus. It was a shrieking, grating sound like claws being dragged across metal. An oval structure became dominant in the scene at this point—an unstable structure that faded and returned again behind the metered tones and the shrieking, a sound I later dubbed "Cat's Claws."

    Then, quite abruptly, it would end, leaving only superimposed images that partially distorted my vision for several minutes and left an unnerving ringing in my ears. I would often spend the next several moments lying awake in the dark, trying to decipher the visions in terms of Jungian psychology. You know, collective archetypes and such. They were wasted moments in retrospect. I was not being haunted by monsters from my subconscious mind. I was being haunted by old Harley himself.

    And so these trances continued in the same manner until the night of Harley's death. I had turned in early that night after reading. Like always, the trance came, but this time I was not visited by images of a smoky netherworld but instead was given a clear view of Harley's basement. Of course, I recognized the room instantly. Harley and I had spent many nights down there playing billiards.

Harley was not so easily recognized. He was standing behind the billiards table, his tired pinstriped suit replaced with a dark robe. He was swaying back and forth very slightly as a tree limb moved on an almost breezeless day, and although his eyes were open, they were transfixed on something only he could see. His large, work-weary hands cradled an antique leatherbound book I now know to be the dreaded *Necronomicon*, a volume of arcane knowledge that contains the testimony of Abdul Alhazred, the mad Arab, and which describes the methods and incantations used to summon demon creatures from beyond to the earthly plane. Harley was chanting over and over again in a guttural tongue: "IA MARRUTUKKU! IA TUKU! SUHRIM SUHGURIM!"

I immediately picked up on the familiar cadence of his speech. It was the same rhythmic pattern I'd heard voiced in murky subtones while I lay helpless in my trances. Faintly in the distance, I could hear a sound like hooks struggling to catch on to a steely surface. Cat's Claws. As the sound grew louder and more desperate, a wavering oval appeared over the billiards table. Upon its appearance, Harley raised his voice until the sound ripped across the small room.

Then Harley met with success. The oval structure that hovered above the billiards table solidified.

It was the entrance into a network of transparent passageways that branched off in all directions as far as the eye could see. Harley's basement wavered, began to lose substance, and was replaced by a chamber with obsidian floors and marble walls that sloped elegantly upward toward a glass skylight. The skylight framed a maroon sky and twin black suns. Masks of a bronze-colored metal hung suspended from the walls.

Harley seemed oblivious to the shifting realities around him. He was staring straight down the tunnel that opened above his billiards table at a large, segmented creature rapidly propelling itself down the tube. *Clakety-Clakety-Screeeeeech!* That's what that ungodly creature's approach sounded like. It ran firmly on scores of legs—*Clakety-Clakety*—and used the two large pincers in its rearmost section to steer and brake through the corridor like a bobsledder—*Screeeeeeeech!*

Harley just stood there and smiled as the thing approached. Smiled! Can you believe it? Can you believe he ever thought that he could control such a thing?

As the horrible demon drew closer, I began to make out its features. It had a waspish, droplet-shaped head that gently sloped down to vicious mandibles. Two large, amber, multifaceted eyes sat above the mandibles, and a third, smaller eye rested on what could conceivably be called the creature's forehead.

I remember watching it all as a third person, knowing I was there in spirit but my body lay in bed in a near-comatose state. I tried to shout,

"Harley! Harley, you old fool, it'll devour you!" I *willed* Harley to hear me. With all my mental strength, I willed my old friend to hear!

My eyes reluctantly opened, and I discovered that I was still in my bedroom, except that now I could see the underlying infrastructure of tunnels, which existed in a dimension parallel to our own but worlds apart. The network branched on endlessly, sometimes traveling through houses or the street, sometimes stopping in midair where it probably connected another plane of horrors to our own dimension.

The whole picture was impossible to take in at once. It froze the blood. It was like watching infinity.

I tore my eyes away from the maddening visage and looked down through my transparent house at Harley's basement and the monster that was rushing toward him. I dove into a tube that led from my bedroom to the flickering coordinate, which was both Harley's basement and an alien stateroom. I fell into the chamber and landed hard on the stone floor.

Clakety-Clakety-Screeeeeeech!

The monster was very close. Harley stood unmoving as if he had always stood there, a Siddhartha awaiting his Enlightenment.

The creature lowered its head and rushed onward.

"Harley! Harley! Move, you damn fool, move!"

Harley turned his head and smiled at me. The creature crushed into him and threw him upward and back. He struck a ripped-up metal wall and fell awkwardly in pain.

The chamber started to flicker and lose substance as the gaudy wallpaper of Harley's basement began to flicker like a transparency over the marble walls and then started to assume depth. I felt myself slowly slipping away. I screamed at Harley to get up, to run, but he lay motionless on the floor, breathing in labored breaths and bleeding from a thousand deep wounds that had been inflicted upon him by his impact with the jagged tears in the wall where the creature had sharpened its pincers.

The creature clattered forward, chittering excitedly.

Enraged, I grabbed a billiards stick from the rack.

The creature pivoted its amber head to fix its three eyes upon me, a stare that would freeze the blood of arctic men. I dropped the stick, my valor replaced by dread. The creature turned back to Harley and began to prepare him for its black maw. As the thing began its tearing, Harley breathed his last thoughts into the ether.

I awoke in Harley's shattered basement and stumbled over to his remains. There was very little left. I remember vomiting, and then I can remember nothing else.

So there it is. I can see that you, too, think that I have succumbed to madness or drink, or perhaps both. But I tell you that Harley used my mind as a mental booster to open some sort of gateway to another dimension, a gateway that would allow the Old Ones to slowly reclaim the earth from human beings. I will curse him forever for showing me what lies out there just under our feet. I stay awake at night, waiting for creatures to tear me into pieces with black teeth and razor-sharp claws. But more than that, I wait for them to pour into our cities and towns and bring the apocalypse on our race.

I stay drunk during the day to keep myself from wondering why Harley would want to bring something like that into our world. Did he think he would find the connection that was missing in his lonely life? Was he looking for power? Perhaps he secretly hated everyone. But that is a hard burden to bear for an old man who once called Harley a friend.

They call me mad, but they cannot explain the condition of Harley's shredded corpse, the crushed furniture, and the slashed paintings. Though they found me there, howling over his corpse, there was none who suspected me of having done that to poor Harley. No, but they do not accept my story either, though they cannot explain how I came to be there and have no evidence of his death upon me. And, my skeptical friend, they cannot explain this.

Lovely, isn't it? Not of this world, at least that's what the local metallurgists tell me. Reminds me of the fearful masks of the Alaskan Eskimos. Here, have a look yourself. There was one just like it that they pulled from Harley's bones, wedged there. They took it away. But this one, well, now that the tunnels are opened, and the house lies empty, I have ventured back, just at dusk, before the creature's wake, and entered the dreaded world and retrieved this. The door has been opened, you see, and only he who opens it can close it.

Ah-ha. I see I've finally started to get through to you. Harley, he's dead; they took his bones away. Now you see, yes? It'll be a slow process at first, but once you realize that death can creep up on you in your sleep, that there's no way to close the door, that you can't even *see* the door, then I'll have you.

You'll sleep less and pick up the habit…I see you're a bit flustered. Do you want a drink? You'll be there soon enough…you'll hear it scuttling just below where we dwell and feel safest, coming for you in the night…every night…never knowing which night will be the night…

Clakety-Clakety-Screeeeeeech

MADAME ZEIST'S PERFUME

Professor James wasn't sure what to expect when he touched down on that small moon in the Orion System, but he certainly didn't expect Madame Zeist.

A probe had returned with pictures of strange ruins on the planet's surface, and as an alien anthropologist, he was intrigued. The most interesting aspect was that two civilizations seemed to have coexisted together on the planet, intertwining their cultures. There were black pyramids and obelisks covered in hieroglyphics, their meaning long forgotten, next to plain stone dwellings that seemed almost Western in nature. Overshadowing it all was a tower in the center. That was the professor's destination.

Upon entering the tower, the headlamp on his space suit revealed crumbling stone blocking the stairs going up, but the stairs that spiraled downward were clear. Climbing down, he encountered an invisible barrier blocking my way. He strained against the barrier and then there was a *pop!* like a bubble bursting as he broke through, and the professor checked the indicators on my suit. Not only was there earthlike gravity but oxygen as well. And even the health monitor flashed green. Any dangerous microbes in the air were now long dead.

The professor removed his helmet, and there was a hiss as air escaped from the seal. He continued and reached the foot of the stairs. Burning torches cast flickering shadows on the wall, and the air smelled stale and ancient. Twenty feet ahead, the corridor opened into a large chamber, and he could hear music and the laughter of a woman.

Professor James entered the chamber. Colorful shards of glass embedded in the walls caught the torchlight, and bottles of every size, shape, and color rested on wine racks at the far end of the room. On the side of the wine cellar closest to the entrance was a large onyx table. Seated at the table were eleven guests lavishly dressed in bright colors. At the head of the table was the host, a striking red-haired woman in a purple gown with a high collar. In her younger years she must have been a beauty, but age had creased and lined her otherwise attractive face. It seemed strange to the professor that the only person drinking wine was the host.

The woman rose and approached him, and the other guests quickly stood up at their places like soldiers snapping to attention.

"Darling, you've arrived! Welcome to my wine cellar. My name is Madame Zeist." Her voice had a singsong quality to it that seemed otherworldly, similar to the music that floated through the chamber.

"I know you have your questions, my dear, but all in due time. You have traveled a long way to find us, so please rest and take a seat," said Madame Zeist.

The guests smiled and nodded as if attempting to put the professor at ease as well. Professor James is an intergalactic traveler who has encountered dozens of alien species. Usually he is extremely cautious in these situations. Perhaps it was seeing other human beings after the cold loneliness of space or Madame Zeist's gracious manner that put the professor at ease.

Then again, it may have been Madame Zeist's perfume. It wafted through the room, pleasant and familiar in a way he couldn't describe. In between sips of amber wine, Madame Zeist would lift up the small pear-shaped jar of perfume and spray it toward the guests. The professor noticed then that the guests would lean forward above their plates and sniff up the aroma, like dogs reacting to the scent of food. The professor was shocked to find himself participating in this odd behavior, and he suddenly leaned back in his chair when he realized it.

"To the twelfth guest," Madame Zeist toasted.

"To the twelfth guest!" the guests replied in unison.

For a fleeting moment, Professor James wondered what had happened to the last twelfth guest that had caused his chair to be vacant, but a second later, the perfume hit his brain and a sense of immense well-being came over him.

Soon, the professor began to have visions. He was drifting through the universe, a being of pure energy without material form. He was filled with joy as he danced across asteroid fields, spun through black holes, and melted into dying suns. He lost all sense of time during his astral projection, and although some distant animal part of him craved nutrition and sleep, this part was overruled by the senses, which simply wished to fly between the stars.

And then suddenly, perhaps due to exhaustion or starvation, Professor James felt himself being drawn back to his body. He saw the planet as it used to be, thriving with two races: one humanoid and one reptilian. And then, as centuries spun by, there was only one race. It was a tall, sleek race of humanoids with scaly tails and forked tongues, and he realized that a horrific mutation had taken place: that which was once human and that which was once reptile had merged.

The next revelations were intimately more personal and, therefore, all the more terrible. First, just before the professor was returned to his body, he noticed a pile of space suits in the corner with symbols belonging to a variety of galactic civilizations. Then he looked around the table. The guests were all skeletons, posed in various positions as if enjoying a feast.

Madam Zeist was smiling at the professor, but her countenance flickered between her former beauty and an evil face with yellow eyes. Lastly, Professor James studied himself. His space suit felt far too big, and his hands were slender and bony. He had to press against his torso to find his ribs, which poked out sharply against his skin.

Just then, Madame Zeist sprayed her perfume, and the horror subsided, replaced by a sense of wellness. She began to laugh, and the professor began to laugh with her, knowing that until the end of his days, he would crave Madame Zeist's perfume.

COMING OF AGE

I now know why children are asked to stay out of the attic. It is not because of rusty nails or rotting planks. It is because there may be something truly terrible waiting in the musty dark for innocence to let it out. It was my grandfather's attic I had been asked to avoid. And last Thanksgiving, I ignored that warning.

It was a family tradition to make the trip around the beltway to my grandfather's house in McLean, Virginia, every Thanksgiving. When I was really little, I used to think it was a castle. Now, with thirteen years of experience behind me, I realize that lots of people in Virginia live that way.

Nobody knew how my grandfather got rich. We did know that he had traveled all over the world and was a renowned archeologist (I'm not sure what renowned means, but it sounds good in front of "archeologist").

How could they expect me to stay away when his whole house was full of neat stuff? In the front hall there was a huge black beetle from Brazil that sat in a glass case. At the base of the stairs, a suit of French armor stood guard. There was a skeleton of a small dinosaur in the living room my grandfather had purchased from the museum, and the study was full of African masks and spears.

"Have yourself a look, m'boy," my grandfather would say. "But stay away from the attic. There are demons up there."

And I believed him. Sometimes, during my explorations of the sprawling home, I would hear thumping from the attic as if heavy boxes were being moved around. *There go the demons again,* I would think with a shiver.

What my grandfather didn't count on was that by the time I was thirteen and corrupted by countless horror films, I *wanted* to see the demons.

I ventured into the taboo zone late Thanksgiving night. My parents had decided to stay over at the house until the next day, and the house was quiet as if the timbers themselves were sleeping. The place smelled of turkey and tobacco smoke from my grandfather's pipe. I tossed and turned, imagining that the beetle in the hallway had escaped its glass coffin and was searching for me with its glossy eyes, slowly working its way up the top sheet to my face…

I fell into an uneasy sleep, and in my nightmares, faceless natives danced around me, their vivid masks backlit by a raging bonfire. I woke up sweating.

I slid out of the damp sheets and walked over to the window. The full moon shone down onto the asphalt street, silvering my grandfather's BMW. In the distance, the highway droned into the night. The lights were on in the house across the street. Two forms gestured and struggled in a silhouette dance, then an arm came across, and the slenderer silhouette fell away from the window. The standing form passed by the window, and then the lights were turned off.

I stepped away from the window, afraid of being seen.

Then, from above, I heard it.

Thump!

I froze. I began to hear my heartbeat.

Th-Thump Th-Thump Th-Thump Th-Thump...

Creeeeeeak!

It was now or never if I was going to meet the demons. I put a hand over my mouth to stifle my quick breathing and entered the hallway. My socks allowed me to creep silently past the knight that guarded the stairs, and I began my ascent toward the attic.

I reached the landing of the second floor and stopped short. A panther leaped toward me, its white teeth gleaming in the darkness! I cringed and covered my face. I waited, but the attack never came.

Looking up again, I noticed that the panther was still in mid-flight, frozen in place. I laughed at my little-kid fear. It was just another piece of old junk my grandfather kept—a stuffed panther.

I continued up and reached the attic door.

Placing my ear against the wood paneling, I waited. Inside, I heard the same woody creaks I had heard ever since coming to my grandfather's house. Finally, after all the anxious, frightful years, I would meet the demons in the attic.

I pushed the door open and entered the dim chamber. I was greeted by a stale draft that smelled like dust and bad breath. I gritted my teeth as I stepped forward through the silky strands of cobwebs. I felt very alert, and soon, my eyes adjusted to the near-darkness.

Yet I could not see the demons. I began to think the sounds I had heard were only rats.

After passing through a mazelike disorganization of large boxes standing on end and passing under a moth-eaten military uniform hanging from the rafters, I met the demons.

The demons were locked in an upright coffin resting against the back wall. Occasionally, the coffin would shift, teeter for a second on a corner, then thud back down to the floor with a small cloud of dust.

There was an Egyptian figure painted on the front of the coffin (I knew it was Egyptian because I had seen pictures of King Tut's tomb in school). The figure's skin was a rich golden color. Two red jewels were set deeply into its eyes.

Cautiously, as if expecting to trip a land mine, I made small steps toward the thing.

Suddenly, the death box propped itself up on one corner, its base scraping across the floor like fingernails against a chalkboard, and fell crashing to the floor.

It landed very close to me. Too close. The jeweled eyes stared at me accusingly. There was a series of short thuds against the cover, and I expected a flood of black ravens to spill out of the coffin and rip me to shreds in the dark, lonely attic where I was never supposed to be in the first place.

I ran my fingers along the edge until I found the crack between the lid and the rest of the coffin. Using both hands, I ripped it open.

Immediately, I was overpowered by a gaseous mixture that spilled out of the box like dry ice. It smelled like Mr. Clean. It burned my nose and made it hard to breathe. I could see a shape beneath the mist.

I turned and headed back for the door, getting tangled up in the old uniform as I tried to make my escape. I quickly pulled the coarse fabric from my face.

Three more previously unnoticed coffins lying on the floor sprang open, and three shadowy forms rose up from them to confront me. Loose bands of fabric trailed from their limbs, and their breath was hollow and wispy, like wind over a desert.

I froze. *Where can I go?* I was surrounded.

The shapes assembled before me, their smiling faces striking me like snakes. There they were, my mother, father, and grandmother, grinning madly at me like it was my birthday party rather than some scene out of *The Twilight Zone*.

I stepped away toward the back of the attic and walked right into my grandfather's chest. I gagged as I got a mouthful of bandages reeking of the Mr. Clean smell. I struggled, but his large, banded arms wrapped around me and held me close.

"Now, now, m'boy. Just relax."

My head began to swim under the bleachy reek and the crushing embrace, and I fainted…

—

I hovered near wakefulness, and voices swam around me:

"Yes, of course, it is difficult at first, Mary. But he will come around. After all, we are giving him eternal life!"

"It really is a lovely gift, Dad."

"Thank you. When he is older, we shall show him the sacred texts of Osiris and the formula for the solution."

I finally awoke to the steady hum of a car engine, and my eyes were greeted with the bland landscape along Interstate 495.

I sat up, and my mother looked back from the passenger's seat.

"So you're finally up, huh, sleepyhead?"

I nodded drowsily and rubbed the sleep out of my eyes. I felt very lightheaded, not dizzy, but literally *lightheaded,* as if my head were lighter.

My dad grinned back at me in the rearview mirror. "Good morning, champ."

My mother started sneezing and retrieved a Kleenex from her purse. I watched as she unfolded the Kleenex to view its contents. There was no mucus, only a small amount of dust.

It was then that I noticed their shallow, wheezing breaths.

"Grandfather gave us a gift for you, son. It's in the back. Have a look."

I popped my head over the seat and glanced into the back of the station wagon. There, glowing golden in the sunlight, was a short Egyptian sarcophagus. It was sort of surreal, that thing sitting there on the tacky green carpet of the wagon as cars streamed around us on the metallic stream that is the beltway. Pearl wisps of vapor escaped from its lid.

With dread I realized that I had been supposed to find the demons. I had come of age. I began to sneeze, and dust particles filled the car's interior. They settled on to the upholstery, and we sped on toward eternity.

THE DAY OF THE CRICKET

I can't remember when I first developed my aversion to crickets and why, even now, I labor with my last breath to betray my own kind. Yes, indeed, I did say crickets—not sharks, snakes, or any other normal subject of common phobias. Crickets, I tell you—not grasshoppers, spiders, centipedes, or even the wildly buzzing, iridescent cicada.

Crickets. Rural Virginia crickets, to be exact, that rise from the lush historical battlefields of the South to assault the ever-expanding border of suburbia. Poe can keep his ravens—if ever there was a manifestation of evil on this earth it comes in the form of those hungry antennae and the unholy black sheen of that exoskeleton.

I know what you must be thinking of me—that I am one of those modern types who squirm at the thought of the tameless masses of beetles and maggots that teem just beneath the dirt, that I am one of those who lie board-straight awake at night dreading the unchecked procreation of the insect kingdom that surges across the globe despite man's chemical attempts to slow its passion.

But we've just met, you see, and that would not be correct at all. I've always loved nature, even the creatures that the popular world deems grotesque. I have knelt on the shoulder of the road outside of Las Cruces, New Mexico, and cradled tarantulas on their journey across the desert sand. I have ventured deep into Appalachian access tunnels to study the brown-black carpet of bats hovering just inches above my head. I have as readily followed the ungainly wild turkey across the mountains of West Virginia as I have trailed the graceful heron across the waterways of Delaware's eastern shore. I had thought of myself as open to nature's diversity—until the night of the invasion, of course.

Despite the lateness of the hour, my arrival at home that evening was not out of the ordinary. It was a still summer night, and as I parked my car and walked down the paved jogging path that skirted a small pond to the patio entrance of my rented basement, I thought of the immense peace of the neighborhood at this time of night, and the beauty of the crystalline brilliance of the stars overhead. Nights such as that one are more easily achieved in autumn when the crisp air burns the lungs and adds a punchiness to the spirit.

The rattle of the keys in my backpack shattered the silence, and I cursed as I searched among my textbooks for the key ring. It was then, in the waning light of the moon as it fell through the thin slits of the deck overhead, that I encountered the horror.

It stood motionless on the corner of the cement pad in front of the sliding door. Its antennae swam in front of its obsidian eyes, and I could sense—please hear me out!—its defiance. How do I know? How do I know that I did not project my own loathing onto this helpless (your word, not mine) creature?

Because we have all been endowed with the ability to sense love from hate, and I had never before sensed a presence so alien and hateful as the one that emanated from that small demon.

For a moment, we confronted one another in the summer darkness.

Chirp! Chirp!

Then it came, and I knew with personal visions more horrible than what a day-lit reality would have revealed that the monster was vibrating its oversized rear legs in hateful harmony as an act of aggression.

In clumsy defense, I threw my backpack at the creature. It tried to scurry off into the high grass that surrounded the patio, but the pack caught its right side. In mad delight, I realized that I had severely disabled the creature, and its sirens had lost their generators. I reached down for my bag and had a nightmarish glimpse of the creature dragging its right leg behind itself into the grass as it left a sticky paste of yellowish matter behind on the cement.

I tore through my bag, no longer concerned about making noise, and retrieved my keys. Once inside, I locked the sliding door and dropped the security bar. Only then did my breathing return to normal. I went into the bathroom and ran some cold water which I splashed on my face, feeling foolish about the encounter as my body began to cool and relax. I placed my hands on the side of the sink, leaned down, and let the water run through my hair.

Chirp! Chirp!

From what vantage point the beast made its assault is still unclear to me, but the telltale prickle of its legs along the small hairs of my neck turned my blood to ice water. I instinctively tried to bolt upward but only managed to bang my head into the faucet. The sudden jerk sent the devil tumbling down my back to where my shirt met my belt, and I felt every pinprick of the beast's struggle to regain its footing. It was enraged, but no more so than I.

I pushed off from the sink and threw myself back toward the wall. I slammed into the towel rack, and there was a sickening crunch and the feeling of something like a crushed crabapple on the small of my back...but a live crabapple all the same: still itching and twitching.

I ran into the bedroom like a man on fire and stripped off my shirt, using it also to wipe clean my back. I balled the whole mess up and threw it into the hamper.

I collapsed back onto my bed and wished for sleep, but I could not shake the sensation of the cricket sliding down my back. I went back into the bathroom, and after a long inspection of the medicine cabinet and behind the area where the wallpaper was starting to peel away by the floor, I started the shower.

I ran the shower for quite some time. The heat seemed to drain out the stresses of the day but could not drain out my terror. I was too paranoid to step close to the shower drain and did not wash my hair for fear of closing my eyes for an extended period.

Once refreshed, I was ready for bed. I turned on all the lights in my room and stripped off the comforter and sheets from the bed. I would lie board-straight across the bare mattress rather than risk the infestation of layers of covers.

My sleep was fitful and interrupted by otherworldly dreams where tall, bipedal soldiers with insectoid heads lay waste to human colonies on the moon's surface. I saw through the soldiers' eyes the horror and sadness of the colonists and felt with a chill the plunderers' cold indifference . . .

You will ask why this next is not also the product of a nightmare, a joyless gift given by Queen Mab while I slept, but no cunning of the gods or endorphin frenzy could dredge up such a scene.

For when I awoke it was difficult to discern me from the crickets. They were everywhere, coating the bed and streaming across me as if I were merely terrain to be traversed. They broke my skin with their coal-black mandibles, hundreds of them imbibing me with their debilitating venom.

My breath was shallow and irregular, and I was paralyzed. Only my eyelids seemed to be mine alone, and I used them hyperactively in my terror to keep the demons from piercing my pupils.

Sweat coursed down my face, and finally, my lightning-quick, terror-driven heartbeat caused my system to drive me into unconsciousness, where even nightmares were sweeter than the waking reality.

It has been said that people can adapt to anything, and during the last few days, I have been tempted to believe them. *Adapt, but not forget.*

My insides are a mess. They slosh around, largely untethered, not supported by any internal structure. The antennae are the worst. It is as if there is a constant ringing in my ears, or whatever I now have as auditory organs. These legs are nothing less than phenomenal. To think that we humans spend our lives on spindly sticks. We think jumping several feet in the air is a marvel! And the sex . . . ah, well, the sex is constant and furious.

But in sum, this is an unwelcome evolution. I must stay focused and ignore the teeming drives of the group. As we forage through these immense and hauntingly familiar townhomes, I realize just how many we have lost now . . . the other we, the we I used to be.

At night I follow the columns of my new brothers outside to the lake. I stand still among them in silence on the bank as they transmit strange frequencies to the cool vibrancy of the stars overhead. My new eyes deceive me; I see patterns of light above respond in rhythm to these alien songs. Perhaps it is simply aircraft coming into Dulles International Airport, barely ten miles away. But these aircraft are silent, if they are aircraft at all. Soon, there will be no turning back, and our brethren will pour from the forests and stream from the sewers in black ecstasy until the Change is complete across America, and then the world.

But not in my house. Not on my block.

As they stupidly seek sustenance, I go hungry in the darkness of the electrical box. Their numbers are so large they do not even notice me missing. Inside the box, I work the wires with my legs and cling to the gathered edge of the curtain I have dragged in to feed the sparks. I am clumsy, but electricity is graceful, like a dancer as it leaps through the air.

Two truths are known to me as I watch the small arc: 1) It is too late for me. 2) I do this not only for myself but for the diversity of nature.

THE SHAMBLERS

The kids where I grew up didn't scare too easily. We grew up watching horror films, listening to heavy metal, and watching our older siblings get stoned. I suppose that's why we enjoyed taunting the old people so much. Our moral compasses were out of whack, and the biggest taboos were, of course, the most exciting.

Perhaps at night, alone in our beds, or at church on Sundays, we knew in our hearts that it was wrong to tease them, just like talking back to our parents was wrong. Having this knowledge didn't keep us from doing either.

It's surprising to me now how much cruelty is carried in teenagers. Having the benefit of several years of reflection, it seems as if my memories are someone else's, that someone else was saying those things and acting that way in my place. But I know that it was simply the madness of youth gone awry in the worst possible way. I didn't just participate in the abuse. I led it.

Though somehow we at least developed the decency to leave the women alone, it was the oldest of the old who were our targets, the ones who should have been in nursing homes but were too damn stubborn to go out gracefully. We never stopped to think that one day we would be in their shoes. I think about that all the time now.

But I am getting ahead of myself.

We called them the shamblers because of the way they walked. A slowed-down half-shuffle that looked almost comical in its difficulty. They all wore the same clothes—plaid trousers (that's what they used to call them—trousers—never pants) pulled up to the waist, thick-soled black dress shoes, short-sleeved dress shirts, thick drugstore sunglasses, and a derby.

The day I remember most was in summer. The shamblers weren't on my mind as I flew down Thacker Way on my BMX bike. The playing card I had clipped in the spokes kept time as I hummed some horrible song in my head, probably Ratt or Quiet Riot or some other '80s drivel that I don't even own anymore. I flew right across the junction of St. Andrews Street without looking, popped over the curb, and cut through the Wilsons' backyard to the woods. The bike path through the woods was complete with several ramps and creek crossings, and riding along it was my newest favorite hobby, aside from sneaking cigarettes with my friends.

The woods whirled past me, and I was exhilarated by the raw speed. I hit the jump perfectly. It was the landing that I missed. My front wheel was turned too much to the side, and I flipped over the handlebars into the brush when it touched the ground. I lay there for several moments, feeling sore in my shoulder but mostly angry at the rookie mistake. The playing card in the wheel ticked for several moments as the wheel slowed to a stop, as if the bike was mocking me. I was just about to get up when I noticed something out of the corner of my right eye.

Remaining still, I cocked my head over to the right and saw one of the shamblers in the distance. The ramp was deep in the woods, and I was surprised to see him way back there. He was looking intently at a briar bush, slowly probing its branches with his leathery hands for a secret goal.

I heard someone approaching and turned to see Charlie and Chris pedaling up to me. "What's up, Tim?" I put my finger over my lips and motioned for them to come over.

"Do you have your slingshot?" I asked Chris.

"Sure. Never leave home without it," he said with a wink.

I nodded. "Good. Get it out."

"Which one is it?" asked Charlie.

"Old man Kensey, I think," I replied.

"How can you tell?" he asked.

"I can't for sure," I replied, loading a nearby pebble into the pocket of the wrist rocket.

I pulled back the rubber straps to their full extension and concentrated on the distant target. There was a whoosh of air as the missile departed. Suddenly, the shambler pulled back his left hand in alarm as if stung by a wasp within the bush's interior. Another pebble grazed his derby before he turned to look our way. Then he began his strange walk toward us, causing leaves and twigs to gather up in the bottom of his trousers.

"Let's get out of here," Charlie whispered.

"Load her up again!" urged Chris.

"Shut up! Let's see what happens."

Suddenly, the old man stopped. He lifted his hand and pointed at me, sending icicles straight to my heart. For once I was happy that he was wearing thick sunglasses so I would not have to directly bear his steely, hateful gaze. Instinctively, my hands combed the earth for pebbles. Old man Kensey started shambling again.

"Uh, guys, he's getting kinda close," stammered Charlie.

"Shut up, wimp. Tim will get him, won't you, Tim?" asked Chris.

I swallowed hard. "Yeah. I'll get him," I replied meekly, searching desperately for ammunition. My hand found something hard and dug it up despite its irregular shape. It could have been a fossilized peach pit for all I cared. I loaded the object into the hungry pocket of the weapon.

Kensey still advanced, the wide bottoms of his trousers making a terrible swooshing sound as he grew closer. My hands trembled as I loosed my bullet. The object hit Kensey square in the sunglasses, and he clawed at his eyes in surprise. That was enough for us. We scrambled over to our bikes and pedaled like madmen out of the woods toward safety and sun and a land without shamblers.

I fear that this narrative will cause you to pass judgment on us, but you must remember that we were just kids. What I mean to say is that it wasn't like we were really out to hurt anybody. We were just trying to have fun in our own twisted, sadistic way. We didn't know about heart attacks or cancer or the loneliness that can come with age. Maybe if we had, things would have been different. Then again, maybe not. I can't explain our behavior, but maybe you can if you remember back to when you were a kid yourself.

When I came home, I locked the front door behind me. My mom, who always seemed to have superhuman hearing, noticed this. "Why the extra security, hon? Is there a prowler in the neighborhood?"

"No. I just thought we should be safe, especially since Dad's at work."

"Are you okay, Timmy? You seem jumpy. Maybe I should make you a sandwich?" she asked. Sometimes I wished she wasn't such a June Cleaver.

"No thanks, Mom. I'm going to go upstairs and read for a while."

She came over and kissed me on the cheek. "Good boy. Let me know if you need anything."

"Okay. Thanks," I said, and vaulted up the steps. I spent many hours in my room blasting through asteroids on my Atari.

I told my parents I didn't feel well when they called for dinner. Finally, after leafing through a stack of comic books, I began to forget about the silent threat issued to me by old man Kensey. My legs were sore from my frantic cycling earlier in the day, and sleep slowly began to tug at me. I began to swing my legs over the bunk to close the blinds when my heart stopped in my chest. Standing on the dark street corner and gazing up through the window was old man Kensey, his arm raised in mute accusation at my bedroom. I quickly jumped off my bed and pulled the blinds tightly shut. I sat there for many minutes by the window, my pulse racing and perspiration beading beneath my pajamas. I expected to hear tapping on the glass at any moment, like in that scene from Salem's Lot. Finally, there was a knock on the bedroom door.

"Are you feeling better, hon?" my mother asked.

"Yeah," I replied.

"Okay. Don't forget to brush your teeth and turn off your light. Remember, bad things come to bad boys."

"I will. Good night." I thought about what she said all night: bad things come to bad boys. I thought about it until my thoughts were replaced by shambling nightmares.

The next day we were up to our same tricks. We had tied a long piece of twine around the base of Mr. Furman's birdbath and were waiting for an unsuspecting bird to land on the small basin. Suddenly the back door opened and Mr. Furman shuffled out, cursing at us damn kids and shaking his cane. We were all the way back at the street sitting on our bikes, and our escape should have been a milk run, but somehow the twine got tangled in my bike chain and I was unable to get going. I did manage to pull over the birdbath while trying to free myself. Chris and Charlie were already down the street and not looking back. Suddenly Mr. Furman's ancient, veined hand clasped my handlebars. I could not have been more terrified had he been holding a fistful of cobras.

"Do you know what I see, Timmy? Do you know what I see when I look at you?" he asked, his rheumy eyes searching my own and his breath reeking of alcohol and cherry wood tobacco.

"N-No, sir," I replied.

"I see me. I see me!" he said. He then began laughing insanely, like a tyrant on the brink of world domination. Ripping my handlebars free and letting my bike fall to the street, I stepped back away from him.

"Don't let them get you, Timmy! Don't let them!" he shrieked.

Suddenly he went silent and hurried back toward the house. I turned around and saw three shamblers watching us from the edge of the woods.

That night, I was determined to discover the secret the shamblers kept in the woods. I decided not to include Chris and Charlie in my quest. Not only would they have trouble sneaking out, but trying to explain to them what I was looking for would cause me to be the brunt of endless jokes. Earlier that night, I had taken the emergency flashlight out of the kitchen drawer. It now rested in my backpack as I carefully climbed down the ivy trellis that was attached to our wall. Soon, I reached the edge of the woods and paused to listen and retrieve the flashlight.

I had spent all of the summers of my youth here in these woods, but I had never experienced it by night. It was alive with small sounds that caused me to madly spin my head in every direction, looking for intruders. I could not use my flashlight until I had safely cleared the houses that backed up against the woods.

Eventually, my eyes got accustomed to the darkness and I was able to begin making my way down the path. I could hear the creek running softly to my right and the summer breeze stirring the creaking tree limbs overhead. After a hundred yards or so, I turned on the flashlight in order to illuminate the roots and rocks that littered the rough path.

I had lost many bike tires to those hazards over the years. Finally, I reached the ramp and paused before cutting off diagonally to the briar patch. Something was dragging itself up the path toward me. I splashed the figure with light and saw a shambler slowly advancing on me, its hand pointing at my heart. I tripped over a root and crawled backward in panic, only to feel my back collide with something solid. I realized it was the legs of someone standing in the path. I screamed out and ran off toward the creek. I took comfort in their slowness and used the flashlight to pan each side of the woods as I ran. I didn't even reach the creek before I spotted another one standing there calmly at the water's edge, smiling a toothless smile in his shades and derby as the light revealed his position. I wildly spun the flashlight around in a full circle.

Shamblers were advancing from all sides, leaving no gaps in their human net. Trembling, I unfolded my Swiss Army knife and waited. Suddenly the back of my head exploded with pain from the blow of a blunt object.

Dropping the flashlight, I fell to all fours and tried to concentrate on keeping my swimming vision centered on one spot on the ground to avoid vomiting from the pain and dizziness. Two shamblers grabbed me by the arms and dragged me over toward the path. I couldn't be sure how many there were. We crossed the path, my knees getting battered on the exposed roots, and continued into the heart of the woods. We finally reached the briar patch where I had initially spied old man Kensey several days before.

Two shamblers were combing the bushes. Mr. Furman was there watching them and calmly smoking his pipe.

"You!" I spat.

"Sorry, kid. I tried to keep you away. We all did."

I tried to rise up to my feet, but the bony hands of my escorts kept me down. One of the shamblers brought something over from the bush.

"Timmy, we are going to put this insect in your mouth. You will not chew it or swallow it. You will allow it to make its way into your system," Mr. Furman instructed me.

"No chance," I stated flatly.

Mr. Furman lifted his cane up and pulled at the bottom. The wooden shaft fell away to reveal a slender blade silvered by the moonlight. Mr. Furman brought the blade up to my Adam's apple and drew a hairline cut.

"You will."

The shambler brought the bug toward my face. I quivered, and the tip of Furman's blade dug deeper.

"Open your mouth," he commanded.

In that terrible instant, I saw the thing they wanted me to accept. It was a spider of rather strange design, with a raised, spiked thorax and red spots running along its underside. My stomach rolled over on itself.

"Do it!" Furman hissed.

I opened my mouth. They dropped it in, and I felt eight alien legs climb down my throat. My escorts held me tighter, bruising my shoulders, as I shook off a gag reflex. After a minute I could no longer feel the spider's passage, and I figured the worst was over. My escorts kept their grip iron-tight. Suddenly my internals were wracked with mind-numbing pain, and I realized with horror that the spider was tearing its way toward my heart. There was a sick warmth in my chest, and I realized that I was bleeding from the inside. I began to cough up blood.

Time itself seemed to stop when the creature's mandibles penetrated the soft, pink flesh of my heart.

There was a brief period of euphoria as the venom radiated through my veins and arteries, providing warmth and a strange intoxication. I thought it was the final release of endorphins from my weary brain before death. But unfortunately, my death was disturbed by a wave of violence far more brutal and terrifying than the first.

My bones cracked and reformed, my muscles tore and stretched, my hair and teeth dropped out. The pain was immense and unbearable. Just before I lost consciousness, a shambler walked over and placed a derby and a pair of thick sunglasses beside me.

My parents think I died that night, and for all intents and purposes, the boy they knew as Timmy did die that night. I've got a new background now, one more compatible with my appearance. They know me at the home as George Tischer, who owned a hardware store in Arizona before retiring and developing Alzheimer's. No next of kin.

It is almost unbearable to live in the same town and not be able to reach out to them, but sometimes I take a walk in the woods and plan a way to get back at the local kids that make my life a living hell.

LAWN CARE

Tonight, a slow summer rain is falling. My muscles are sore, and I sit on my back porch and smoke a Marlboro, releasing the day's tension and feeling renewed by the cool drizzle. I had almost achieved some fraction of nirvana when my next-door neighbor Larry disrupted my reverie.

"Okay, Jack?"

"Yeah. How the hell are you, Larry?" I tried to sound enthusiastic but knew it came out forced.

"Fine, just fine." He removed a Macanudo cigar from his tacky Century-21 blazer and lit it. A cigar is a long smoke; Larry planned to be out here with me for quite a while.

I knew it was coming. 10 . . . 9 . . . 8 . . . 7 . . . 6—

"You know, Larry, I could help you spruce up this backyard of yours. I've got some extra seed out in the shed. The grass is already dead on those yellow patches."

Up yours, I wanted to say. "Thanks, but I like it just fine."

"Okay, but don't say I didn't warn you. The Homeowners' Association is looking to crack down on lawns this year."

I said nothing. It was always the same with Larry. It was always about making my yard look better so I wouldn't be a blemish on the neighborhood. But I knew it ran deeper than that. Larry thought that I personally was the stain on this row, a freak, a forty-year-old piece of white trash that followed NASCAR and drove a motorcycle. I had denied him the chance to have one more golf buddy, to have the ability to dump his wife onto the neighbor's wife while "the boys" went out to the country club.

I knew he hated me for that. And although that really wasn't my thing, I hated him too for making me feel like all those things about me were true.

"Funny thing, summer rain. So slow and deliberate. I liken it to a well-ordered life. Slow and steady wins the race, I always say. Know what I mean?" he asked.

"I prefer storms," I replied blankly.

Larry took a large drag on the cigar and let it out in a smoky puff that hung in the air like a sigh. I knew what he was thinking. *Poor white trash Jack. Why won't he let me help him?*

For several moments the light hush of the rainfall continued, and we sat in silence, two neighbors separated by more than property lines. I could tell I made him uneasy, and he snuffed out his smoke before it was half done. This brought me wicked satisfaction.

"Goodnight," he said, ambling back onto his own property and opening up the sliding door.

"Goodnight," I replied half-heartedly. "*Asshole*," I added as he closed the door.

Finally, I was alone again. The townhouses run back against the woods, and it was easy to forget about the modern world here in the cool silence. I could hear the creek running into the hungry drainage pipe behind the trees, and for the moment, the big ugly airplanes with their intrusive lights and rumbling turbines were strangely absent.

I'm not normally superstitious, but I have a healthy respect for man's sixth sense. So when goosebumps rose and raced along my damp skin, I knew I was no longer alone in the yard. I held my breath and studied the woods, looking for the pair of alien eyes I was sure were looking at me. I thought I saw something amorphous and large along the ground—slithering along the ground—but then I was sure it was only the tangled outline of stumps and briars.

It was then that the soles of my feet began to grow warm as if they were resting on beach sand, and looking down I spied the strange intruder. It was a worm, or at least I think it was a worm, but it was the strangest worm I had ever seen. Three stalks with luminous green bulbs swayed above the sinuous body, and it vaguely resembled a picture I had seen of the lantern fish that live in deep ocean trenches. It was only about two inches long, and aside from the curious antennae, its body was surprisingly wormlike.

But the real difference, the horrific difference I mean to say, was the way in which it regarded me as I regarded it. Despite charges of insanity I must nonetheless confess that it regarded me with intelligence.

It was then that one of the soft globes brushed my bare ankle. I felt an instant sting, like placing your skin against wet snow. I instinctively jerked back from the alien touch, and the creature shot across the grass and then dived into the earth like a glowing drill bit.

Had I been drinking, I would have dismissed the entire incident, but I was stone-cold sober (and wishing I wasn't). That had been no ordinary worm, and when I looked into the trees, the mass I had mistaken for stumps and briars had disappeared.

That night I had strange dreams. I squirmed through muddy concourses with thousands of my greasy brethren, their chemical lanterns like a thousand will-o'-the-wisps guiding my way. Although I felt extremely disoriented in the close darkness, I had been imbued with the knowledge that we were moving upward toward the surface. We forded underground rivulets and the dens of small animals, finding pockets in the earth like a seamstress feeling for a thread. I felt a great hollowness in my new body that I attributed to hunger, but although the earth moved and teemed around us with beetles, roly-polies, and spiders, none seemed to attract my invertebrate senses.

Finally, we seemed to have reached our goal, for the column of worms had been reduced to only two wide up ahead. Twisting and rolling nearer, I noticed an opening of wood, and I thought that we were entering the floor of some poor bastard's home.

I was dead wrong. Upon entering the chamber, I was instantly overcome by an overpowering, sickly sweet smell. My twisting and squirming seemed less productive than before, and I noticed I was now traversing a strange pink fabric that caused my viscous body to burn as I rolled against it. The smell, whatever it was, seemed to overpower me and impassion me beyond normal hunger. There was a horrible slurping sound and I knew by instinct my brothers were feeding.

As the column widened, I saw the goal. Hundreds of the worms scoured the corpse, devouring flesh, bone, and marrow. The smell in the air, the candy I craved, was death. And I was in a coffin.

I awoke violently, thrashing and rolling and not yet aware that the bodies we inhabit in dreams are not our own. Then I was still. The clock on the night table read 2:05 a.m., and I was comforted beyond description by this simple electronic device because it meant I was truly back, not trapped in a worm's body or a coffin or a snake's den or an underground river but truly back to my old self. I turned on the lamp and allowed my pulse to slow.

Perhaps the venom from the worm's bite caused hallucinations. Perhaps I was still freaked by the whole thing. Either way, I needed a beer. I was about to rise and make my way downstairs to the kitchen when I heard something outside. It was an intermittent munching, like a rebellious rabbit raiding a vegetable garden. I didn't have a garden.

I silently crossed the carpet to the window and looked down behind the house. The scene was breathtaking, a mechanized dance of small green ghosts that drew a phosphorescent grid across my lawn as they worked, regurgitating nutrients for fertilizer and mowing down the towering weeds. I rubbed my eyes and they were gone. Only the glowing green trails they had left rested briefly on the lenses of my eyes, and then nothing but a vacant backyard.

I turned away but something caught the edge of my vision, and looking back I saw a green glow burn briefly in the heart of the woods before an amorphous mass crept out of sight. Doubting my own sanity, I turned away from the window, went downstairs, and proceeded to get drunk.

—

The doorbell sounded like an air raid siren, and I sent Olympia beer cans spilling across the table as I jerked awake. The rattling of the several renegade cans against the floor caused my head to hurt even more.

"Christ!" I muttered, rising and pulling my robe around myself. *Who would come knocking this early on a Saturday? Certainly no friend of mine.*

I wearily unlocked the deadbolt and pulled the door back. The bright sunlight caused me to squint. Larry was standing there in khakis and a plaid shirt, smiling like Ward Cleaver. This neighborly crap was getting to me bad.

"Yes?" I asked defiantly.

"Sorry to bother you, Jack. I just had to know—how did you do it?" He seemed giddy or obsessed or something. Definitely not the same old boring Larry.

"Do what?" I asked.

"C'mon buddy, don't be sly. The yard! It looks wonderful. In fact, I'm a little envious. Why, just last night it looked like he—well, I mean, it's such an improvement."

"Larry, I don't know what you are talking about."

"Okay, okay. I can see you don't want to talk about it right now. Promise me we'll talk this afternoon."

"Sure. Whatever." I began to close the door.

"Jack?"

"Yes!" I was exasperated and hungover to boot. A deadly combination.

"I don't know what you did, but I'm glad you did it."

"Yeah. Okay. Thank you," I replied, closing the door and relocking the deadbolt. I looked out the window to make sure he was leaving, and he tipped his Derby hat. *What the hell has gotten into him?*

I walked back to the kitchen and began picking up the scattered cans. I was unusually hungry, and I began to cook up some scrambled eggs and sausage. I ate ravenously, and only after scraping off the dishes and rinsing them in the sink did I get a chance to see just what Larry the Golf Pro was talking about.

Overnight, the lawn had been transformed. The grass was not only green, but it was also verdant, thick, lush, and beautiful; the type of lawn that makes you want to take a blanket outside and set up a picnic lunch. The yellow patches were gone, replaced by a sea of swaying emerald blades. It was several inches high, cut to even height, and perfectly trimmed along the edge of the porch.

I stood in my tattered blue robe under the blue sky and white cumulus clouds and laughed. I had the one thing that Larry wanted. As I laughed, the soles of my feet began to grow warm.

—

I didn't see Larry much over the following months. He tried, incessantly at first, but I told him my lawn simply had gone crazy one night and decided to grow. He told me that it wasn't very neighborly of me to lie to him, and finally, in a fit of frustration, called me a sonofabitch outright for withholding the information. He didn't matter much to me. I had been imparted with the ancient and all-knowing knowledge of the earth, and this knowledge had changed my life. Mathematics and other subjects that had been previously unfathomable to me became instantly clear, and soon I was able to make enough money that I hired several workers to perform the fireplace installations while I supervised, placed advertisements, or found new business. I had traded in my Ford F-150 pickup for a Dodge Stratus and had purchased several pairs of dress pants and collared shirts.

My friends called me a sellout, but I didn't care. Don't ever let anyone tell you that money can't improve your station in life. I was able to buy things out of want for a change rather than need. I was dating women who wouldn't even have looked in my direction before. Life had been transformed from a tart apple into a juicy peach. But still…

Still, there was the hunger. Hunger that made my bones ache, hunger that made my heart rattle in the ribcage. No amount of sex or sustenance could satisfy me. I longed for sleep and the dark dream-journeys through the earth. Like an addict, it was taking more to get less. I was working a six-hour day and sleeping an eighteen-hour night. People asked me if I was ill. My skin now had a frightful pallor and suitcase-sized bags burdened my eyes as if threatening to pull the surrounding skin oozing down my face. I joked about partying too much or sitting behind a computer all day, but people were beginning to talk.

I was burning out, slowly losing the handle of balancing real-world responsibilities with my newfound addiction. It was time for desperate action to prevent a total breakdown.

—

Larry Moore was used to winning. It wasn't easy to lie in bed and forget something like that. He was the leading realtor at Century 21 as well as having the distinct pleasure of having the lowest golf score at the office. And until recently, he had had the greenest lawn on the block.

He couldn't explain the transformation of Jack Marshall, but he knew it wasn't just a blue-collar boy overcoming his roots. He had known self-made men and Marshall just didn't fit the mold. It had all happened close to the time that Jack's normally weed-infested plot had bloomed into beauty. He didn't know the connection, but he was determined to find out.

He had been watching and had witnessed the strange phosphorescent bands of light that seemed to bind Jack's turf together in the dead hours between midnight and morning. He had seen Jack disappear into the trees with the moon overhead as his sole companion, only to return pale and drained in the dawn.

Tonight he would find out why. After his wife had fallen asleep, Larry carefully extracted himself from the sheets. He looked down at the still form of his wife for a moment and felt a twinge of guilt for sneaking around like a teenager after curfew. He touched her cheek in a genuine show of affection and then began to get dressed.

The fact that the urgings were getting worse came surprisingly easy to me. I rose groggily from my dreams and slipped on a pair of tennis shoes.

My little glowing friends were already churning their way across the backyard by the time I reached the patio door. I stood behind the glass and watched them for a moment.

It somehow continued to awe me. I wondered if they derived any joy from their furious activity, if they smiled as they surfed through the waves of grass, or if they simply carried out their task by genetic instruction, mindlessly, like spawning salmon.

I opened the door and they immediately scattered, some diving into the moist earth while others skipped away toward the woods.

I winced as the pain came again. It was deep in my forearms, buried in the marrow of the bones, a writhing agony like a corkscrew slowly spinning through sinew and muscle.

I had learned to ignore it like I had learned to ignore so many things lately. It was a testament to the human soul how the abnormal, even the freakish, becomes mundane.

Taking a quick look at the surrounding townhomes, I noticed that not a single window showed light. Would it make a difference? Could a junkie put down a heroin needle as it hovered over his hungry vein, even if a cop was standing in the alley with him?

There was a distinct crispness in the August air that reminded Jack of autumn as he made his way along the wide, paved path that wound through the woods behind the development. By day it was a bustling thoroughfare of joggers and bicyclists, but now it was dark and silent except for the gurgling of the creek that ran beside the path. The darkness became overwhelming once he was embraced by the cover of the trees, and Jack paused for a moment while his eyes adjusted. He had the distinct feeling of eyes on his back, and he spun around only to be greeted by silence and a breeze.

Having gained his night vision, Jack continued for another several minutes down the path and then broke off into the woods toward the creek. After fifty feet or so, he reached the water's edge and used a half-rotting oak that had fallen across the creek to cross over to the other side. He had learned from experience that the going was easier on that side.

Around him, the small noises of nocturnal foragers could be heard as he made his way down the muddy banks. He was worried about stepping onto a nest of copperheads this close to the water. He thought about the thin line between civilization and wilderness, between sanity and madness. If he was insane already, how would he ever know?

He tried to dismiss such thoughts as he made his way under the moonlight. The creek split off in two directions: one way following the original course parallel to the jogging path and another into the heart of the woods. Jack followed the secondary stream into the woods. When he first started coming here, he hated this part of the walk because the woods became much denser here and the thick briar patches would cut his exposed skin.

Now, the shallow scratches were a pleasant distraction from the deeper pain that writhed within his flesh.

Suddenly there was a movement behind him and Jack paused. It had been a shuffle of leaves, like a broom sweeping stiff bristles across a sidewalk. The small creatures of the forest have a way of walking at one with the woods, silently, like a soft rainfall on the leaves. This was different; larger, clumsier.

It sounded like a man.

"Hello?" Jack asked as he slowly turned around, slightly amused at the thought of someone else wanting to be a part of this dark journey. He couldn't see anything, but he sensed that he was not alone. The human part of him found this comforting. The new part of him did not.

Larry crouched low behind a tree. He was uncertain why, but he felt true fear at being discovered by Jack. It was more than the fact that he would be required to provide an awkward explanation. Somehow he was sure that harm would come to him. It was irrational, as fears tend to be. Although Jack had developed some strange behavior over the last few months, Larry had no reason to believe that he had become violent.

It may have been the lateness of the hour or the psychological effect of the dark woods. Whatever the reason, he held himself completely still at his position. Larry couldn't shake the eerie feeling that Jack knew he was being followed.

After Jack was out of sight, Larry continued, cursing under his breath as he was cut by dead branches and thorns along the way. He was cold even in his sweat suit and longed for his warm bed.

But he longed for Jack's secret even more. He had theorized for weeks that Jack's secret was not a brand of fertilizer or pesticide but rather something natural, some simple herb that no one had ever tried before. Something that could make an ambitious man of enterprise such as himself very rich.

His intent was not to interfere. He just needed to get close enough to identify the plant that Jack was utilizing. After all, Jack seemed in no hurry to patent the formula; why should the rest of the world suffer? Developing this product seemed the right thing, the democratic thing.

Or at least that's what Larry had told himself a hundred times over the last couple of days to justify his behavior. In his heart he knew it was stealing someone else's hard work to make up for his own lack of knowledge. It was no different than breaking into a competitor's office and Xeroxing their client files. But he had learned a long time ago that nice guys finish last, that the ends can justify the means.

There was a glow in the trees up ahead, and as fear crawled over him, he clumsily made his way behind a fallen log to avoid being discovered.

Jack slid diagonally down the muddy embankment. *There is a cycle to everything in life,* Jack thought to himself, a circle that begins with death and ends with death—in between, there is only the hunger and the feeding. This thought came instantly to him, without precognition, but somehow he knew it to be the coal-black bedrock behind the worthless enterprises of man. The brain is not separate and apart from the spirit but chemically married to it. And as the body changes, the brain and spirit are transformed as well.

There was another clumsy movement behind him in the woods, and Jack knew that whoever it was that had been trailing him was still close behind. It did not matter.

The creek ran into a large sewer pipe. The entrance was high enough that Jack could enter it by slightly stooping as he walked. All around him, the hyperactive worms burst forth from the creek and flowed into the sewer, their greenish glow now bright white like a thousand miniature flashbulbs going off all around him. The light they provided showed the normal strange assortment of junk that can be found in sewers everywhere: old shoes, cans, baseballs, and the almost required pornographic photos torn from cheap magazines for juvenile delight. Suddenly, the organic light dissipated, and Jack was left alone. He was trembling, and the muscular living cables inside of him resettled once again, racking him with spasms and causing a cold sweat to break out across his body.

Jack heard the sloshing approach of his pursuer by the entrance and continued on deeper into the sewer. The faint beam of a flashlight soon appeared behind him. He picked up his pace until he reached a four-way intersection where the main pipe joined another. He turned right and tried to make himself flat against the wall. His back writhed and contorted. The invertebrates within him could sense the dampness of the hard surface and wanted out. Jack bit his lip and was silent for what seemed like an endless repetition of pain.

Suddenly the light from a flashlight illuminated the sewer floor beside him. The stranger stepped cautiously past Jack's position. Jack sprang at the unwelcome guest ferociously, grabbing his shoulders and forcing him facedown into the low water and grime. There was a moment of intense resistance and then gagging as the stranger's nose and mouth filled with the sludge-like fluid. Jack rolled him over after several moments.

"Jesus!" the man gasped. In that single word, Jack's suspicions were confirmed. He did not need the flashlight to know that it was his neighbor Larry. Jack released him, and Larry recovered his flashlight.

"You shouldn't have come here," Jack said flatly. Larry flashed the light up at Jack, and Jack covered his eyes. The worms beneath Jack's skin flexed sharply as if they had been scalded.

Larry felt revulsion at Jack's physical appearance. He was like an animated corpse, with stringy hair and deep-set eye sockets that could easily have been empty in the near-darkness. Larry swallowed his nausea and put on his best salesman's voice.

"Jack, I'm not unreasonable. I want to be your partner. Together we could become millionaires with this product!"

"What product!"

"The lawn care product, what else?" Jack replied.

"You shouldn't have come here. You really, really shouldn't have come. I'm sorry about this."

"Jack, don't be angry with me. We're neighbors. I'm not asking for the rights or anything . . . hell, you can even keep the damn formula. I just want a piece of the action, an investment between friends."

"I'm really sorry you decided to do this. I'm really very sorry. Tell Sallie I'm sorry."

"Why do you keep saying that?" Larry demanded.

"Look, forget it. Can I just see the flashlight? I need to show you something."

"Sure."

Jack grabbed the flashlight. It felt smooth and well-balanced in his hand. It would work. Jack smiled and blinded Larry with the light. Larry half-smiled and blinked, unsure of himself. He probably did not even see the blow coming. Larry fell heavily into the sludge.

I used Larry's belt to tie his hands behind his back in case he came to while I waited.

Thin streams of blood began to flow down my arms where the skin had begun to tear.

The worms needed to be fed again. They needed to be fed soon or they would consume me.

Suddenly I heard it off in the distance. Somehow, hearing it before seeing it was the worst part, and I clicked on the flashlight for a sense of safety. Sometimes I thought it sounded like a thousand souls in agony. Other times I likened it to a thousand steam valves being released at once. Most often it just sounded like animals spontaneously decomposing.

Soon the concrete walls of the sewer began to pulsate in the distance with a green, alien glow, and I could make out an amorphous shape slithering toward me. Eventually, the quivering mass was in front of me, its rank stench assaulting me and its three eye stalks regarding me with alien disregard. It was the Lord of the Worms, and it had come to hold court. Thousands of the phosphorescent worms teemed across and within its body, giving it a radioactive aura. One of its sinuous appendages had fused a used syringe onto the end of itself, and somehow this modern implement made it all the more menacing.

The syringe was filled with the glowing substance. For once, the worms inside of me were still with anticipation. Although I had come here for my nightly fix, Larry had given me another option, and maybe this way, I would live.

I dragged Larry's unconscious body over in front of the Lord of the Worms. In unison its three eye stalks sprang back, and it emitted a thin hiss. I held my hands out in front of me and stepped back several steps to show that I meant no harm.

I shivered as one of the sinuous appendages flashed out and rested on my forehead like a wet feather. The tunnel began to spin around me, and I placed one hand on the wall for support. I heard Larry's scream as the syringe was plunged into his heart and watched the shimmering forms of the worms gleefully spring from their host and invade his mouth until he could only gargle. His mouth glowed with the unholy light, and I was grateful I was losing consciousness. I could hear the sickening crunch of the worms burrowing through my flesh toward freedom, the dreadful vacuum as they decoupled from my brain, the silent slip as they uncoiled from my ribs.

I should have endured hellish pain but was numb. Before I lost consciousness I swear the Lord of the Worms paused before me and laughed. My last image was of the creature continuing on its way down the passage, dragging Larry's limp body behind.

I do not think that I will be visited by the worms again. It is almost autumn, and I have not seen the strange glow in the woods or the nocturnal coils of energy binding my grass together. I sometimes wonder how far the sewers go, how many other neighborhoods they connect to, and if, somewhere, somebody else is living the nightmare all over again. I have gained some weight back, and despite the scars and the aches in my joints, I am once again healthy. My grass is back to its half-dead state, and I have lost my heightened energy and intelligence along with my newfound fortune and friends. Larry's wife and I have married, and it is nice to once again live a normal existence.

Despite the approaching winter, Larry's grass refuses to give up the ghost. It grows lush and green as if powered by an unknown energy. Life is a circle, and everything comes to completion. I wonder sometimes if he waits beyond the trees for me and what it would be like to go with him. For now, I avoid the woods and the storm drains. I recently purchased a clock radio with giant amber numbers that help me with my nightmares. Life is a circle, a circle that repeats, and perhaps that is the real tragedy.

R. DAVID FULCHER

R. David Fulcher is an author of horror, science fiction, fantasy, and poetry. His major literary influences include H.P. Lovecraft, Dean Koontz, Edgar Allen Poe, Fritz Lieber, and Stephen King. Fulcher is the author of several collections, including *The Light-house at Montauk Point and Other Stories* and *The Pumpkin King and Other Tales of Terror*.

His work can also be found in the anthologies *Hard-Boiled and Loaded with Sin* (Hawkshaw), *Halloween Party 2019* (Devil's Party), and *Halloween Party '21* (Gravelight).

More at rdavidfulcher.com

ACKNOWLEDGMENTS

I would like to thank David Yurkovich and Dianne Pearce of Current Words Publishing for their assistance on this manuscript and on many other of my literary efforts.

RDF

If you liked ASTEROID 6, don't miss the companion volume,
THE PUMPKIN KING AND OTHER TALES OF TERROR.

MIDWEST BOOK REVIEW praises Fulcher's collection: "Reminiscent of Poe and other masters of the macabre, R. David Fulcher's collection of creepy tales relies more on psychological surprise than gore, tapping the inner sense of what makes a subject terror-stricken in order to deliver its power. Take the opening short story in this collection, 'Marienburg Castle,' for example. Seasoned horror genre readers simply won't expect the opening lines of this story: At first, they were mere specks in the sky. The specks became white wedges, like falling pieces of creme pie. Closer still, they appeared as marionettes, dancing with umbrellas across the horizon.

Fulcher excels in the unexpected, and as the story unfolds, his penchant for description and atmosphere continues to excel: The cathedral hovered directly before them, its stained-glass windows shining like jewels in the moonlight. The castle stood adjacent to the church, silent and dark, sealed behind thick iron doors and high barred windows. They ascended a stairway onto the battlements and stared out into the night-enshrouded valley. "Holy Jesus!" muttered Walker. The woods surrounding the keep were filled with small pinpoints of light. These observations drive events that lead readers to the dark side of a group of soldiers that face an unexpected a battle far beyond their training, playing out beyond death itself.

Readers of all ages should anticipate not just thrills from seemingly common and uncommon events, but the excitement that stems from a close attention to building exquisite tension, atmosphere, and a one-two punch of surprise to keep readers guessing about outcomes."

Don't miss THE PUMPKIN KING AND OTHER TALES OF TERROR, a Gravelight Press collection. Available in multiple formats at Amazon, Audible, and finer bookstores.
gravelightpress.com

GRAVELIGHTPRESS.COM